After the Stroke of Midnight

By Jennifer Lewis

For Mia,
and in loving memory of her
fairy godmother, Olga Marina Martinez,
who made her so many
beautiful dresses when
she was little.

1

"I have a surprise for you."

Sandy startled at the sound of a voice and looked up to see Conchita, the nighttime cleaner, next to her cubicle. "What do you mean?"

"It's a ticket." Conchita waved a piece of paper in her weathered hand. "To adventure and excitement."

Sandy laughed. The canned promise sounded extra phony in Conchita's heavy accent. "I'm not sure I can handle much more of that. I just scored two new customers in Singapore."

"You're a clever girl, but too young and pretty to sit here night after night. You're going to a party." She shoved the paper at Sandy.

Who squinted at the letters in the dim light of the almost-empty sales floor. The page proclaimed its holder the winner of a magazine's charity fundraiser, a raffle that had been advertised a few weeks ago. "It's a ticket to a date with Marco Danieli." Sandy looked up at Conchita, whose green eyes gleamed with enthusiasm. "He's the owner of the company."

"I know." Conchita beamed. "Soooo handsome!" She blew a kiss to the air. "If I was younger I'd date him myself."

How sweet of Conchita to think of her. But really!

"I can't go." Why would Marco Danieli want to spend an evening with a nobody like her? "And read the fine print. It says here that employees and associates of Danieli Electronics can't enter."

Conchita snorted. "Nonsense. Who better for him than someone who already knows and appreciates him?" Sandy smiled. Marco Danieli wouldn't know her from a hole in the wall. She was just one of thousands of anonymous employees.

"And what would I wear?" She gestured to her jeans and T-shirt. "I don't exactly have a glamorous wardrobe."

"You need new clothes. First impressions are important." This was quite a statement coming from a tiny woman in a faded housedress.

"I'm trying to save money."

"Don't worry." Conchita's grin creased her wrinkled cheeks. "I already made you a dress."

And that was how Sandy found herself in Conchita's tiny walk-up apartment on the afternoon of the date. With grandmotherly warmth, Conchita applied scorching heat to Sandy's hair and pulled it hard with a brush, taming her wild curls into a sleek fall.

"I don't know how you did that." Sandy stared at her own reflection. "I look like a totally different person."

"In my country we know how to do hair." Conchita winked. "Now the dress." She clapped her hands together and rushed to the closet. Sandy held her breath while her new friend fumbled among her dowdy housecoats. Whatever Conchita brought out, she was going to wear it. The sweet older woman had gone to so much trouble and effort already.

Conchita pulled a hanger from the back of the closet and twitched out a long midnight blue dress with a subtle sheen to the fabric. She held it up for Sandy to admire.

"It's beautiful."

"You're beautiful." Conchita smiled and pulled the dress from the hanger. "And you'll be even more beautiful in this dress."

Sandy dressed under Conchita's beady gaze and was both surprised and relieved to find that it fit perfectly. "I was a seamstress for many years at the top bridal salon in Santo Domingo."

"That's where my mom was from," exclaimed Sandy, before she could stop herself. She didn't like to talk about her mom. She didn't even really remember her.

"I can see her Dominican beauty in you." She squeezed Sandy's cheek so hard it made her gasp. "You just need a little magic to bring it out. Turn around."

Sandy twirled, and the skirt gathered elegantly about her legs. It was fitted but easy to move in. Conchita produced a pair of vintage-looking silver stilettos and helped her into them. "Come look."

Teetering precariously on the high heels, Sandy approached the dingy mirror on the back of the bathroom door. A woman she didn't recognize stared back at her. "Wow."

Conchita beamed. "Marco Danieli won't know what hit him."

"Wait, I almost forgot!" Sandy made her way back to her bag and fumbled in it for the tiny box that held her blue contact lenses. Her dad had given them to her as a disguise for some shady deal he'd planned.

She'd refused to participate—finally grown a backbone by then—but she'd been fascinated by how they looked so she'd kept them.

She stuck them awkwardly in her eyes, one by one, and blinked. The transformation was complete. With blue eyes, straight hair and at least four more inches of height, Sandy knew even her own father wouldn't recognize her.

If her dad were still alive, he'd have wanted her to go tonight. He'd never cared one bit about following the rules.

Marco Danieli would have no idea he was on a date with one of his own employees, or that she was just a lowly salesgirl from the graveyard shift.

"Where's my coach with white horses? Do we need to catch some mice?"

Conchita laughed. "You'll have to take the subway, princess. I have plenty of fabric and thread, and the shoes were once my favorites, but I don't have money for a cab."

Sandy kissed her on both cheeks and descended the six flights of stairs to the street. There, she drew in a deep breath of New York City air and headed for the uptown train.

Sandy caught sight of Marco Danieli sitting at the hotel's upscale bar, alone, severe and elegant in his trademark dark suit. His black hair was combed back, emphasizing the hard lines of his handsome face. He wore the habitual serious expression that intimidated business rivals and employees alike.

Sandy's heart pounded against her ribs as she approached him. Every nerve ending in her body tingled with the thrill of coming face-to-face with the object of her fantasies.

"Mr. Danieli?" Cool and casual, greeting a stranger.

"Yes." He looked up. Steel-gray eyes met hers and sent a delicious shiver of fear mingled with anticipation skittering along her spine. "Miss Alma?"

"Please call me Alexandra." Her real name, though no one ever called her anything but Sandy. Alma was her middle name. Tonight she would be Alexandra Alma, confident, assured, sexy, and hopefully irresistible. Everything Sandy Riley was not.

"Call me Marco." He stood and gently placed his hand on her shoulder. He pulled her close as he rested a soft kiss of greeting on her cheek. Hope bloomed along with a quick flush of heat where his lips met her skin.

For a single instant, all the blood in her body rushed toward that one electrified spot and she thought she might crumple to the floor.

But her knees held firm.

"May I get you a drink?" His low voice wrapped itself around her, and she groped for the words to respond.

"White wine, please."

He turned away from her to order, and she gulped a breath. Her body still tingled with the afterglow of his polite kiss. Already she felt sensual, a little wanton. She consciously threw back her shoulders and held her head high. Sandy Riley might not be able to carry off a date with a man like Marco Danieli, but Alexandra Alma was more than equal to the task.

As the waiter poured wine into a chilled glass, Marco gestured to the velvet-upholstered stool next to his. Sandy slid onto it as gracefully as possible, hooking her impossibly high heels over the base.

"I can see I should donate my time to charity more often," said Marco. His cloud-colored eyes darkened as they swept down to the plunging neckline of her blue dress. The appreciation in his face warmed her in dark, secret places.

"It is a good cause, isn't it?" She smiled politely as the bartender handed her the wine. "I don't buy dates with strangers."

Truer words were never spoken.

"I've never done this before either." Marco sipped his drink and looked at her steadily. A coil of desire twisted in her gut. "And I think we should make the most of it, don't you?"

"Definitely." She smiled what she hoped was a bewitching smile, raised her glass to his, then took a sip of the cool, golden liquid.

Classical music tinkled gently in the air around them. Clear notes mingled with the soft clinking of glasses and the low chuckles of contented guests in the opulent surroundings.

"You probably know who I am, since you bought a raffle ticket for a date with me, but I don't know anything about you other than your name. Do you live in New York?"

"No," she said with a shrug of regret. No lie there. She was a Jersey girl born and bred. "I'm from out of town. I'm here on business."

"What kind of business are you in?"

"Marketing." Which sounded so much better than telemarketing. "The work brings me to New York from time to time." Every workday, in fact.

"I'm glad it did." His sensual mouth curved with the hint of a smile. He lifted his glass. "Here's to all the forces of the universe that brought us together tonight."

A thrill of promise warmed her as she clinked her glass gently against his and raised it to her lips.

She'd thought a lot about what she would say tonight. How she'd talk to him. She knew he dated a lot of women. She'd been reassured to see that he'd dated a black girl before. Still, the others were beautiful models and actresses, women who could entrance a man without lifting a finger.

She couldn't hope to outshine them so she'd devised a different strategy.

And it was time to put the plan into action.

"If you could have three wishes, Marco, what would they be?"

Marco turned to face her, an eyebrow raised in surprise. "Are you a genie?"

"You never know. I might be." She felt a bit like a genie. Had she conjured that sparkle in his eyes?

"I guess I'd have to wish for world peace." He winked at her, a gesture that made her heart jump. "Otherwise I couldn't look myself in the face every morning."

"A wise choice."

"As for the second…" He paused, lowering his eyes to graze her body, claiming her with his cool and commanding gaze.

Sandy responded by leaning slightly toward him. The silky fabric of her dress slid over her thighs as she crossed her legs. As she waited for his response to her daring question, she tasted a new kind of power that she'd never imagined.

"My second wish might be happiness for myself."

"Hmm." Sandy raised a finger to her lip,

considering. She lifted a doubtful eyebrow and watched his lips move into a curious smile. "That's a bit vague. What exactly constitutes happiness for you, Marco?"

He spoke casually, but his eyes darkened. "If I knew that I'd be a rich man indeed."

"You are a rich man."

"I won't have to waste a wish asking for riches." He sipped his drink and set the glass down hard on the counter, looking into the swirling clear fluid as if it were a crystal ball. She saw him retreat into himself, lost in thoughts she had no way of understanding.

To the casual observer Marco Danieli had all a man could want, but who knew what hopes and dreams he kept to himself?

"Happiness is an elusive goal," said Sandy, trying to regain his attention. "The more you chase it the further it runs away. Who said that happiness is what happens while you're busy doing other things?"

"I don't know." His eyes searched her face as if she might have the answers he needed. Her heart squeezed. If only she did.

"Asking for happiness is too easy. If you ask for happiness, then it must come along with all the other things you always wanted."

"Unless you're the lucky soul who's content with his lot in life."

"I don't think many are, do you?"

"I suppose not." Marco took another sip of his drink. A shadow passed over his face as he studied his glass again.

She was losing him! So much for bringing him out of his shell and enchanting him with her wit and perception. She'd driven him deeper inside it. Perhaps intellectual stimulation wasn't the best way to a man's heart. What did she know?

She shifted in her chair and leaned forward to lift a napkin off the bar, offering a daring view of her cleavage in the low-cut dress.

Nothing.

Oh dear.

She decided to try another tack. "What do you say we get out of here and go somewhere a little more lively?"

He looked up at her and nodded. "Sounds like a good idea."

"Is there anything you'd like to do? Maybe something you enjoy that you haven't done in a long time?"

Marco lifted a brow. "How do you feel about jazz?"

"I love it." She smiled at the look of surprise on his face. Most people her age hated jazz, if they even knew what it was. But she'd been raised on it.

"I know a place in the Village. We can get dinner while we're there. Do you have a jacket?"

"No." She'd half hoped they wouldn't leave the hotel. Movement brought complications. A twinge of anxiety tightened her chest as she realized what she'd started.

She'd have to retrieve her gym bag with her work clothes in it from the ladies' room and bring it with her. Either that or come back for it later. Since she had to be at work by midnight, getting back up to midtown and over to Chelsea would shave a good hour off the time she had to spend with him.

And she wasn't willing to give up a single second of her dream date.

"I have to grab my bag. I'll be right back." At least the bag was black and not too obtrusive. She tried to pretend it held important business documents, rather than jeans and sneakers.

Marco waited for her as she attempted to saunter elegantly across the bar in her unaccustomed heels. He smiled and extended his arm as he walked toward her.

"Give me your bag."

"Oh, no, really, it's okay."

He cocked his head and looked at her through narrowed eyes. "Hand it over, lady."

She smiled and gave him her bag. He slung it over his shoulder, then offered her his arm. She took it gratefully, glad of any assistance in remaining upright.

As Sandy walked across the gleaming marble floor of the hotel lobby, arm in arm with Marco, a thrill of pleasure warmed her from head to toe. She caught a glimpse of their reflection in one of the mirrored columns and saw them as any bystander might: a glamorous couple out for a night on the town. She and Marco Danieli.

In the cab downtown Marco rested his powerful arm along the back of the seat, brushing the top of her shoulders. The night was warm, dark already, and the city flashed by in a blur of light and sound. The cabdriver played Indian music, and the repetitive drumming echoed the pounding of Sandy's heart as her body jostled against Marco's in the tight space.

Marco relaxed against the seat, smiling at the people who hurried along the busy streets as they drove down into the Village. "I used to come and listen to jazz all the time, but lately it seems I'm stuck uptown listening to piped-in classical music at tiresome galas."

"I know what you mean," she lied. She smiled at him. "It's hard to find time to do what you enjoy when there are so many demands on you."

"That's it. You work hard to get established, looking forward to all you'll be able to do once you're successful."

"And then once you're successful, you're too busy to do the things you looked forward to."

"Exactly." His eyes drifted toward her, and she saw a curious expression twist his unsmiling mouth. She wasn't sure if she imagined it, but his arm seemed to slide a little lower on the seat back, draping itself casually over her shoulders and sending a heat wave coursing through her body.

Marco's legs were too long for the cramped space in the back of the cab, and they stretched a little into what she thought of as her space. His knees brushed hers and little frissons of electrical energy jumped from body to body, through the tailored fabric of his pants and the soft silk of her dress.

She was aware of his body beneath his clothes, the skin beneath the suit. They bumped and lurched through the bustling streets, the air conditioning inadequate in the summer heat. Or was it the rapidly rising heat of two bodies too close together? Marco's skin released an alluring hint of aftershave that taunted Sandy's senses. She was far too conscious of the raw masculinity coiled and waiting in the elegant figure of the man beside her.

The cab jerked to a halt outside an understated storefront. Marco paid the driver and helped her exit the cab as graciously as possible in her high heels.

"This is the place." Marco smiled when she looked doubtfully at the battered doorway. "Good food and music you can dance to. And a low profile to keep out the riff-raff." He winked at her.

He opened the door and led her along a dark, featureless corridor. If she hadn't been so confident of Marco's reputation, she might have been nervous. But when he opened another door, they emerged into a room reminiscent of a sleek 1920s jazz club.

The air throbbed with music. A small band filled the stage, and the saxophonist jammed out a rousing solo that pierced the air and caused a smile to spread over both of their faces as they warmed to the atmosphere of this secret world.

"Come on, let's get a table." Marco placed a hand at the base of her spine. The effect was anything but steadying. Sandy sauntered across the floor, her body unconsciously keeping time with the music. She noticed people looking at them, looking at her. For someone used to flying under the radar, it was alarming and exciting.

She didn't hear Marco give his order to the waiter, and was surprised when he returned with a bottle of champagne.

"Let's celebrate," he said, raising his sizzling glass. "To unexpected adventures."

"And magical summer nights."

The bubbles tickled her nose. She'd drunk champagne only once before, at the retirement party for her former manager. A hesitant sip from a plastic tumbler in a florescent-lit conference room. Hers had not been a life where champagne flowed freely. Not much had flowed freely, except tears.

She wondered what Marco would think if he knew

she wasn't a glamorous international businesswoman, but a girl who'd just barely survived to adulthood on a steady diet of grim determination and escapist fantasy. She was only twenty-four though she knew she looked older. Wise beyond her years for all the wrong reasons.

The candle flame danced in his eyes as he put down his glass and reached out to her. "It seems a shame to sit here when we could be dancing."

She took his hand, warm and firm, and rose from her chair. She floated toward the dance floor on the music that jumped and shimmied through the air around them.

The band was playing an old Count Basie number and the steady rhythm tickled their feet into a dance almost before they reached the small parquet dance floor. Marco slid one arm around her waist and took her hand. He looked steadily at her face, his eyes daring her to look away as he moved to the music.

He was the first to break their staring match as his eyes dropped to her cleavage, then down over her torso, where the blue silk clung to her slim body. One good thing about never knowing where your next meal was coming from, you didn't get fat.

Sandy, don't dwell on the past! Live—right now—in this present that feels like a dream. Was it a dream? Her imagination was so vivid and well exercised that sometimes it was hard to distinguish between fantasy and reality.

Then she stepped on Marco's foot.

"Sorry!"

"That's okay." He steadied her with the strong hand that held hers. "You can walk all over me if you want. I might enjoy it."

He smiled. He let his gaze roam freely over her body as he twirled her gracefully and caught her again, squeezing her just a little. Possessive. She could see desire in his eyes, darkening the gray like gathering storm clouds. She wondered if her own desires were so visible through the shaded blue of her contact lenses. Probably.

Her body was melting wax in his hands, so warm, fluid with excitement as they moved to the complex rhythms and the sharp blasts of a trumpet solo.

She'd practiced, watching old movies, wrapping her arms around herself, and skipping across her tiny room. And she'd danced with the best. Ralph Riley, the Hummingbird, named because his feet moved so fast you could hardly see them. Her dad.

The Hummingbird wasn't moving so fast by the time she came along. His addictions had already gotten the better of him by then. But every now and then the old fire flared up and the Hummingbird whirled into action, flying through the air, taking his partner on a trip to the moon and back without leaving the confines of their cramped basement apartment.

Dancing was in her blood. Along with all that other stuff.

She was rusty and out of practice, but she could feel the unused muscles springing to life as she and Marco cut a new groove across the wood floor.

"You're some mover." Marco's eyes shone with a mixture of admiration and pure male lust.

"Thanks, so are you."

And he was. Maybe dancing was in his blood, too. Something they shared. An affinity that could bridge the vast chasm between them, at least for the duration of a trumpet blast.

They stumbled back to the table breathless, hot and excited by their exertions, and Marco poured them both more champagne.

It seemed so decadent to quench her thirst with the bubbling liquid. She had no need for intoxicating stimulants. The air around her swirled with unspoken desires.

People were watching them. Sandy sensed their eyes swiveling toward them and jumping away. Seeing an attractive couple in the first blush of love? She didn't know what they thought—but she felt their admiration and enjoyed it.

Living in a dream world was safe, controlled, the ups and downs neatly defined by her wishes and fears. Living in the real world was a gamble and now she spun on the roulette wheel not knowing where it would stop.

"What made you buy a ticket to spend an evening with me?" Marco looked genuinely intrigued. "When I signed on for this date, I thought I'd be escorting a grandmotherly owner of multiple cats out for a waltz or two. If I'd known what was in store, I'd have volunteered more readily." The heat of his admiring gaze threatened to singe her skin.

She wanted to laugh. Conchita had three large tabby cats. "No good deed goes unpunished."

"I'll take my punishment like a man."

He was a man, all right. Big, broad shouldered, seething with raw sexuality. She could almost taste his desire for her as she watched him lounging easily in his chair.

"And what kind of punishment did you have in

mind?" she teased.

"Definitely more dancing with you."

Her insides tickled with anticipation of the pleasure. With Marco Danieli she'd be glad to dance all night and into the morning.

No chance of that, though.

"And what if I keep you dancing until your shoes wear out?" she asked, smiling.

"I hope you'll keep me dancing until I'm ready to fall to my knees."

"And then you'll beg me to stop?"

"I'll beg you to punish me just a little bit more." His steely gaze dared her to contradict him. Dared her to take him up on his challenge.

"That sounds dangerous."

"Sometimes you have to live dangerously." His eyes flashed a warning.

She was living dangerously, all right. She could lose her job for this.

"You would know. You built a billion-dollar company in less than ten years."

"You know more about me than I know about you."

"I only know what everyone knows."

Marco leaned forward, resting his elbows on the table. He let his glance drift across her cheekbones and down toward her lips, which parted in involuntary response to his mute appeal. His eyes narrowed slightly. "And what does everyone know about you?"

"Very little, and I intend to keep it that way." She smiled and sipped her champagne.

She was mysterious by necessity. No one really knew her, no one ever had. The ugliness of her childhood had kept her at more than arm's length from other people. She was an object of pity if they thought of her at all. No one ever knew what secrets she carried in her heart.

Now that she was grown, independent and free of grim obligation, she still kept her own counsel out of habit. She didn't know how to relate to others in the easy, friendly manner that seemed to come so naturally to everyone else. Concealment and secrecy were second nature to her.

She'd lived above and below the law. She would carry that shame to her grave. The way her father had carried his guilt to his. And perhaps worst of all was her guilt that she hadn't loved him enough to save him.

"There's something to be said for mystery," said Marco softly. "It never disappoints."

"Have you been disappointed?"

"Haven't we all?"

She looked at him. His expression revealed nothing, the hard lines of his face conveyed no feeling, but the gray darkness of his eyes swirled with emotion. What secrets did Marco Danieli carry in his heart?

"To hope is to risk disappointment."

"And what do you hope for?" Marco's voice lowered, husky with desire.

"To enjoy the rest of our evening together."

And then to take home my memories, share them with Conchita, then wrap them in cotton wool and treasure them.

"To that end, let's order some dinner."

They ordered fondue. A dish for lovers or intimate friends, dipping into the same pot to share the bubbling liquid. Sandy half wondered if they would feed each other, offering tasty morsels of meat across the snowy expanse of the tablecloth. But they didn't.

He was guarded, too.

Perhaps that was part of the reason Marco Danieli intrigued her. He had an aura of mystery, of unspoken secrets. She supposed that even the richest men in the world carried invisible burdens. But it wasn't her place to uncover his secrets. Just as she wasn't willing to share her own. That was why tonight was all they had.

She sneaked a glance at her watch. Only one hour left before she'd have to leave for work. Magical as this night was, she couldn't risk losing her job.

Again he led her onto the dance floor, where the music had slowed with the lateness of the hour. Marco pulled her into a gentle embrace that made her body hum with pleasure, and they swayed together to the soft thrumming of a double bass and the tinkling of piano keys.

He inclined his head toward hers and she listened for his whisper but none came. Their conversation was silent, a communion of bodies, of the parts of the mind that no one understands.

Marco's fingers slid over her back, kindling embers of desire wherever they went. Her hips swayed to the mellow rhythms of the music as they moved, slow and easy, across the dance floor together. The throbbing bass echoed the rhythm of her blood as it moved through her body, bringing the intoxicating chemistry of emotion, attraction and desire to her fingers and toes.

They were building a fire together.

She let her hands trail up his shoulder and over the collar of his shirt. Her fingertips reached up to his neck, touching the prickle of his cropped hair, the male roughness of his skin. He didn't protest. He bent his head toward her, sharing his breath as their mouths came perilously close.

His fingers explored the twin hollows at the base of her spine and teased the upper curve of her buttocks. The warmth of his skin penetrated the thin silk of her dress and she wondered if the dress itself might simply evaporate, just as the room fell away, along with the other people in it. There was nothing in that moment but her, Marco and the music.

She let her other hand slide inside his jacket and around to the firm muscles of his back. She ran her fingertips over the soft cotton of his shirt, enjoying the hard ridges that lay beneath and pulling him closer.

The tempo quickened. Whether it was the music that came first or the heightened pace of their twin heartbeats, Sandy couldn't say. All she knew was suddenly they were whirling across the dance floor, turning, twisting, groping and grabbing at each other.

Their legs stepped this way and that, weaving in and out of each other in a tango of impossible passion. Their bodies itched to touch each other, impatient of the clothes that kept skin from skin.

When their lips met, the world exploded into a crescendo of stars, coupled with a clash of cymbals, as emotion and passion climaxed in the melding of their mouths.

Her tongue hungrily sought his. They clutched each other and their feet stopped moving as they gave themselves over completely to the soul-stirring magic of their kiss.

Marco's mouth moved over hers, greedy for it,

tasting and possessing her. Her hands gripped the sides of his face, holding him close. Her nose brushed against his, changing sides with it, changing back, as each sought to deepen the kiss, to make it more than any kiss could be.

At that moment the music stopped and the room burst into applause.

Sandy and Marco fell back from each other. Sandy was dazed and amazed as the polite clapping continued. The applause seemed to celebrate their kiss, and perhaps it did, even as the band took their bows.

Marco led her back to their table, weaving through other couples as they applauded the mastery of the musicians. Sandy eased into her seat, painfully aroused. Her nerves sang with longing she'd never imagined.

Marco's gray eyes were dark with passion, his face taut with emotion. He took her hand as they sat at the table. He looked as if he was about to say something, but words didn't rise to his lips.

There were no words for what had just happened between them.

Her dream had become a reality, and so much more than a dream could ever be.

More pleasurable.

More exciting.

More terrifying.

Sandy covered her confusion in a sip of water. Her girlish game of flirting had gone further than she'd intended. She'd implicated Marco in her fantasies, drawn him out and aroused him. She'd treated him as a phantom, a fantasy lover without feeling, but he had responded as a man.

As she replaced her glass, her eyes rested on her watch. It was eleven fifteen. To reach work on time, she had to leave within the next five minutes.

Marco reached across the table and took her hand. He placed his other hand over hers, rubbing it gently. The heat from his skin mingled with hers, a friction creating sparks as he continued the oddly primitive gesture.

At last he spoke. "You've bewitched me."

She swallowed. Perhaps she was a witch with dark powers capable of entrancing this man she admired so much. Of bringing him harm.

"I didn't mean to."

"You never asked me what I wanted for my third wish."

"No," she half whispered it. What he wished was none of her business. Her little game seemed risky now it had gotten so far out of hand.

"I know what I want now." His voice was quiet yet assured.

She remained silent, afraid.

"I want to know you." His eyes searched her face, seeking the knowledge he asked.

No, you don't. You want to get to know the woman you think you see. The sleek-haired, blue-eyed woman in the shimmering silk dress.

Her heart clenched with the sorrow of it.

She didn't speak.

"Will you see me again?"

He wasn't trying to take her home, to seduce her, to claim her for his bed. He wanted to meet again, to talk, to pursue a friendship that could lead to who knows what.

What a shame it was impossible. More than

impossible.

She had to leave. *Now.*

"I have to go to the ladies' room." Not a graceful exit but all she could think of.

Marco nodded silently and released her hand from his. Her fingers were suddenly cold out of his protective grasp. She tried to walk gracefully across the room, teetering in her high heels without his arm for support. Her head spun, emotions whirling out of control.

It was over.

A perfect evening. More than she'd imagined, more than she'd ever dreamed. And now it was done. As she left the main room of the club, she saw the ladies' room but hurried past it. Rushing, fumbling, she retrieved her bag from the coat check and ran outside into the cool night air.

There was no moon. The streetlights and the headlights of passing cars lit her way as she clattered along the pavement lugging her heavy bag, shivering in her thin blue dress.

Alone.

2

Sandy ducked into the McDonald's on Sixth and West Third, making for the bathroom. Late night coffee-drinkers barely lifted their eyes as her heels clicked across the tiles.

In the cramped space of a stall, she shrugged out of the silky dress and kicked off her heels. She slid a gray long-sleeved T-shirt over her head and pulled on familiar faded jeans. Herself again.

She groped in the darkness of her gym bag, looking for her sneakers, but could only find one. Even as she emerged to the florescent-lit row of sinks, it didn't materialize.

Ugh. One expensive Nike sneaker gone. Even though she'd bought them on sale, it was still thirty-five dollars down the drain. Reluctantly she slipped her feet back into the high heels.

At the sink she removed the blue contacts, then tugged her hair back into her usual ponytail and used water to scrub away the last traces of eyeliner, mascara and lipstick that had outlined and enhanced her features.

The transformation from princess to drudge was complete. She didn't have any fireplaces to sweep out, but she had cold calls to make. Customers in Asia waited to hear a hard sell on the wonders of Danieli Electronics while America slept.

She slipped out of McDonald's and dashed across the street to the subway entrance, on her way back to her ordinary life.

The trains were slow at that hour and she had to wait. Heart thudding and her breath labored, she ran the blocks from the 23rd Street station to the converted warehouse near the water that housed Danieli's offices.

She shoved inside and took the stairs two at a time, bag banging against her back and her heels ringing on the metal staircase. She crashed through the door, ripped her time-card out of its slot and punched in.

12:03.

Another five dollars docked from her paycheck.

"That's the third time this month, Miss Riley," the shrill voice called from the open door of the manager's office.

"I know, the train was delayed."

"Excuses don't pay the bills." Her new manager was a hard-nosed shrew who'd probably never been a single minute late in her life. She certainly showed no mercy. But Sandy was good at what she did and they both knew it. And from now on she wouldn't have any reason to be even one second late. She needed this job too much to make any more mistakes.

Marco waited patiently as the minutes ticked by. He topped up their champagne glasses. He requested a dessert menu and wondered whether Alexandra would prefer flan or chocolate mousse. He enjoyed the renewed music as the band started up their second set.

But as five minutes became ten, as ten became fifteen, he turned and stared in the direction of the restroom with increasing frequency.

After twenty minutes he became angry. What the heck was she doing in there? After thirty he was worried. Maybe something happened to her?

Apprehension clawed at his gut, souring the taste of the champagne. Where was she?

At midnight he strode across the floor. He rapped hard on the door of the ladies' room, then flung it open.

"Alexandra?"

A startled middle-aged woman paused in the middle of reapplying her lipstick and gave him a dirty look.

"No one in here but me."

"Sorry." He let the door close and stood in the hallway, wondering what to do next. He was baffled. How could she just disappear like that?

He approached the coat check. "Did the young lady in a blue dress pick up her bag yet?"

"Oh yes. I'm glad you asked." The boy with spiked hair and multiple piercings turned away and retrieved something from a bin on the floor. "She dropped this as she was leaving. It fell out of her bag."

He handed Marco a single sneaker. Pale blue with white stripes. A little worn and scuffed.

"I figured she'd come back for it, but I guess you can give it to her now."

The words sank in, leaving Marco stunned, dazed. She'd left him.

She'd slipped away without even a polite goodbye.

His fingers tightened around the single sneaker.

Why would she do that? And why would she do it to *him*?

As far as he could tell they were having a great time together. Damn, more than great. A sudden flashback to their kiss illuminated his imagination. The spark of memory withered with the realization that she'd left him with no way to contact her.

She'd skipped out on him. Left him high and dry.

And he wasn't going to let her get away with it.

He didn't want revenge. He didn't entirely know what he wanted. But he knew he had to see her again.

"I'll be right back for it." Back at the table, Marco paid the bill, tossed back the last of his champagne, and bid a wistful farewell to the evening he'd enjoyed so much.

If anyone wondered why a tall man in a black suit was striding along Fifth Avenue at midnight, carrying a single blue sneaker, Marco Danieli was totally unaware of their concern.

The following night Marco was twisting under his sheets, sleepless and irritable at 2:00 a.m. when his phone rang. He groped for it in the dark.

"Hello." He usually only got calls this late if there was a major emergency: a shutdown at one of the factories, a power outage halting production, a massive system failure or data loss. He sat up in bed, bracing himself for bad news.

"Marco." A woman's voice. Low, so soft it was almost inaudible.

"Yes."

There was a pause and he racked his mind for who his late night caller could be. He wasn't seeing anyone right now and he was fairly sure none of his recent girlfriends would be delusional enough to try to reawaken his interest.

Then it hit him.

Her.

"Is it you?"

"Is it who?" The soft voice teased. He imagined a smile playing around the corners of her sweetly seductive mouth.

"Alexandra."

A tinkling laugh danced along the phone wire and into his ear, taunting him. "Would that be your wish? You can call me by any name you choose. Or you don't have to call me any name at all."

"A mystery woman."

"Your mystery woman."

Marco shifted under the covers, aroused already. "Where are you?"

"Wherever you want me to be."

"I want you to be right here, with me."

"In your bed? It's very late." The husky voice was agonizingly seductive.

"Yes." His affirmation was hoarse.

"Are you alone?"

"I am."

"Are you wearing any clothes?"

Marco looked down at his rumpled undershirt and boxer shorts, which were barely visible in the green light from his clock radio. He considered the situation for a fraction of a second before replying. "No. I'm not wearing any clothes."

"Good. Because they'd get in the way of what I'm going to do to you."

Marco was intrigued and dangerously aroused. And not accustomed to being a liar. He pushed down his shorts and hiked his T-shirt up over his head. He maneuvered his shirt swiftly around the phone receiver, not wanting to miss a single word from his alluring caller.

He reached behind him and raised the window blind a little, looking out at the dark and uncharacteristically quiet city. Rays of moonlight fell into the room, pooling on the crumpled sheets of his bed, glazing his bare skin.

"Why did you leave me?" he asked, curiosity overcoming his anger at being abandoned at the club. "I need to see you again."

"Needing, wanting is a risky game." Her throaty voice tickled in his ear.

"Yes."

"It can make you crazy. Make you do things you never thought you'd do."

Like undress for a phone call? Marco wasn't used to taking directions. He was more comfortable calling the shots.

But now his naked body ached with desire.

"What did you think you'd never do?" he asked.

"I'm not sure." She paused. Silence hummed along the phone line. Then a whisper. "But I think I fell hard for a man."

Her voice was so soft that the words seemed to slip into his ear and disappear before he had a chance to grasp their meaning. Then he wasn't sure if he'd heard them at all or just imagined them. Dreamed them.

In the silence, Marco tried to picture the woman at the other end of the phone. He tried to see her dark hair falling softly over her shoulders, the smooth line of her chin, her high cheekbones. He tried to picture lashes lowering over her unusual slate-blue eyes. But the image proved elusive.

"What man?" The hesitation was audible in his low voice.

"A man who can never love me."

Was she talking about him? Love was not a subject for casual conversation. For Marco, love wasn't even a subject for consideration.

Unless you believed in love at first sight.

And over the past day, and half a sleepless night, he'd begun to wonder if such a thing was possible. Whenever he closed his eyes he saw visions of her shapely body. He imagined her soft lips slightly parted, begging for a kiss. Soft dark hair trailed over his face in waking dreams that kept him permanently on the brink of arousal.

But she was right. Marco Danieli had loved once, and he would never make that mistake again.

"Why can't this man love you?"

"Because of who I am."

"Who are you?"

"I'm a dream. A dark secret that can never see the light of day."

Marco tried to picture Alexandra Alma in daylight, the sun sparking highlights in her hair, but he couldn't. Moonlight was her element.

"Have you ever been in love, Marco?"

"A long time ago."

"And it didn't last?"

"No." His answer was curt. Anger always flared when he remembered he'd been duped, betrayed. Anger at himself.

"So you know love is just a temporary illusion. A delusion. A fever dream that will fade and leave you cold and alone when the sun rises."

"That's for damn sure." He wasn't proud of the bitterness he still harbored. But it protected him.

"Who was the woman you loved?" The voice was barely above a whisper.

"Why do you want to know?" Suddenly he was suspicious.

"Because I want to know you, Marco. And your secrets are safe with me. I'd never use them to hurt you."

Marco rubbed a hand over his face and raked his fingers though his hair. Was she for real? A seductive lover-confessor daring him to open up to her?

He should slam the phone down. He should put his damn shorts back on and go to sleep.

But somehow that was impossible.

"Who was she, this woman you loved?"

"My wife." A long silence. He listened hard, wanting to hear movement at the other end of the line, wanting to confirm that there was a person there. A real human with a beating heart and muscles that could move and ache.

He heard nothing. His phantom caller waited.

Waited for further confessions.

And he made one.

"My wife left me."

His disgust still made bile rise in his throat. Even after all these years.

"Broke your heart?"

"Yup." He scratched his head. He never talked about his marriage. Or his divorce.

Never.

Anyone who knew him knew better than to bring it up. The biggest disappointment of his life. The kind of disappointment that cast a long shadow over all the days that came after it. That sucked the color and joy from simple pleasures, mocking happiness as a temporary delusion.

"We were married young. She was my first love." A hollow chuckle rose in his throat, choking him. "My only love."

"Even a taste of love is a precious gift."

"That kind of gift I can do without."

"She hurt you badly."

"You could say that. She ran off with my boss. The guy who owned the garage I worked at. Left me out of a wife and a job. She told me she left me because she knew I'd never amount to anything and she was tired of being poor."

A harsh laugh shook him. He did enjoy the irony of it. "She picked the wrong sucker that time, didn't she?"

"It looks that way."

"Not a patient girl, Deanna. She didn't think anyone other than me would care about improved acoustics in car stereos. She thought I was wasting my time fiddling around with wires and woofers and tweeters, trying to come up with a prototype."

"History has proved her wrong."

"Indeed it has. Did you know one of my acoustic setups was on the last probe to Mercury?"

"I didn't. Your reach extends to the stars."

He laughed. "I never thought of it that way. But hell yes, it does."

He glanced out the window, looking for stars, but the hazy glow of streetlights and the illuminated windows made them too faint to see.

He wondered if his caller hid in one of those

shadowy buildings out there.

"Where are you?"

"I'm right here." Her whisper sounded so intimate he could almost feel her warm breath on his neck.

"Stop teasing me."

"Oh, you don't mean that." He heard a smile in her voice.

"Don't I?"

"I'd like to tease you a little. If you'll let me."

"Do I have a choice?"

She laughed. A soft, rich sound that caused a reverberation under his skin.

"Not really, Marco." He liked the intimate way she whispered his name. "Not when I can put my tongue inside your ear, when I can lick around its delicate shell, when I can take your earlobe in my teeth and gently suck on it."

Marco felt a sympathetic tingle in his ear, as if her tongue really were traveling through the airwaves to caress the tender flesh.

"I want you to roll over so you're lying on your belly." The cool voice commanded him softly and he obeyed.

He didn't know what the hell he was doing, but it felt good.

"Good."

Could she see him? It wasn't possible.

"I'm behind you."

He battled a strong urge to turn around.

She laughed.

"No, you can't see me. I'm with you in spirit but not in body. But if you concentrate hard you'll be able to feel my fingers as they trail along the hollow of your spine."

The small hairs on the back of Marco's neck prickled as he imagined soft, cool fingers sliding over his skin. He buried his face in the sheets and gave himself over to the imaginary sensation.

"I could climb over you, lie on you and press my body against yours."

Marco imagined the warm pressure of a woman's body on his back. Breasts, belly and thighs embraced him while a woman's arms slid over his, covering him, claiming him.

He flipped onto his back and sat up. She was taunting him. Tormenting him. Adrenaline surged through Marco as he considered just hanging up.

But he didn't.

"I need you," the voice said softly. Hesitant. "And you need me."

"Why exactly do I need you?"

"Because you're lonely."

"I've got people milling around me all day. And all night now that you've woken me up. A little peace and quiet is what I need."

More silence, then the voice was quietly controlled.

"Your wish is my command. Good night, Marco."

A little click and the line went dead.

Marco looked at his phone. He put it to his ear and listened.

Nothing.

She was gone.

Good.

He put the phone on the nightstand and eased onto his side, then pulled the sheet up over his nakedness. Suddenly a cloak of moonbeams didn't seem adequate cover from the prying eyes of the city. He lowered the blinds, shutting out the constellation of electric lights that illuminated the night.

His T-shirt and shorts lay on the pillow next to him and he flung them onto the floor.

What kind of madness made him undress for a voice on the phone? Lord only knows what he'd do next. Maybe he did need a woman. It had been a long time since he'd given dating a serious try.

Alexandra had shown real potential. Beautiful, intelligent, and a businesswoman who'd be able to relate to his busy schedule. And he liked the strange questions she'd asked him.

Three wishes. But what use were three wishes if she couldn't make them come true?

Marco rolled back onto his stomach and pressed himself into the mattress, willing away the erection that still taunted him.

It wasn't easy being a man.

Sandy adjusted her headset and surreptitiously looked around her. The floor was almost deserted. There were only three callers on the graveyard shift, and her supervisor was in her office with the door closed.

She could hear the quiet murmur of her coworkers as they spoke into their headsets, communicating with people on the other side of the world. Their voices weren't loud enough for her to even tell what language they spoke.

She couldn't believe she'd really called him.

She'd found his phone number on a classified company list she shouldn't have access to and written it down. Stored it in her wallet. A secret charm. A possibility too dangerous to act upon.

Until she'd acted upon it.

Had he truly been naked? Or had he lied? Had he undressed himself just for her?

By the time she hung up he'd been angry. She'd intruded on his privacy.

He'd been with her for a few moments, though. He'd wanted to talk. Wanted to tell her his secrets.

No good came of being the confessor.

In the morning he'd regret telling her. He'd associate her with the shame of his divorce. He'd hate her for knowing.

But that didn't stop her from wanting to know more.

Home in bed, Sandy woke up to a strange pulsing in her body. Muscles contracted without her will. The muscles that embrace a lover in the most intimate way possible.

Her obsession, her passion, was extending even into her dreams.

And she knew she had to see him again.

3

Sandy suppressed the urge to tiptoe as she walked across the unfamiliar marble lobby of the corporate offices. Each footfall echoed off the marble walls, a bold announcement of an arrival that filled her with trepidation.

When she'd phoned the club to ask if they'd found her missing sneaker, the attendant told her they'd given it to her male companion.

To Marco.

How humiliating that he should have her smelly old sneaker as a memento of their time together. A time she'd abruptly ended when she dashed rudely out the door without saying goodbye.

Her heart pounded like a jackhammer when she called his office to ask about her sneaker. She could have lived without it. She could have bought another pair.

Maybe he'd be too angry to give another minute to the woman who'd walked out on him. But just as she couldn't resist calling him, she couldn't resist trying to see Marco again.

Leaving him had crushed her spirit a little. Their kiss had stolen her breath and deprived her of good sense. She'd felt a connection with Marco that she couldn't explain in words or thoughts.

She knew it was wrong to want someone so unattainable, someone she was so wrong for. But that didn't stop the wanting. Curiosity and desire made her reckless.

And there was Conchita. Her cheeks had grown pink with delight as Sandy recounted the details of her magical evening. She gripped her wrist with a gnarled hand and begged her to find him and retrieve her sneaker. Was it right to disappoint a sweet old lady?

She'd phone his office and Marco's secretary had answered. Oddly, she'd known all about the sneaker. And she'd insisted, as Sandy had both hoped and feared, that she come in person to retrieve it.

Reluctantly Sandy had once again let her Dominican fairy godmother demonstrate her skill at blowing out curly hair and styling a Jersey City girl into a sophisticated woman. She half wondered what would happen if she showed up as her everyday self but wasn't brave enough to find out.

"Miss Alma?"

The middle-aged woman pushed her glasses up her nose and rose from her desk, as Sandy emerged from the elevator. "I'm Dee Landers. We spoke on the phone earlier. Mr. Danieli is waiting for you."

Sandy swallowed hard. She'd hoped—even assumed—that he'd want to see her, but she had no idea what she was going to say. How he would react to her after she'd walked out on him? Suddenly this whole plan of coming to collect her sneaker seemed insane.

Even her using the ticket to an evening with him wasn't in flagrant violation of the contest rules, she'd abandoned him in the club. If he found out she worked for him he could have her fired, or demoted to part time work without benefits.

She needed this job and the tuition reimbursement that came with it. Without it she'd never finish college and get her life on track. She needed so badly to leave the past behind. She wanted to build a worthwhile life for herself. A life above reproach, built on her own accomplishments.

She'd kept her head down for so long and worked so hard, and now she was going to throw it all away over a sneaker?

No, not over a sneaker.

Over a man.

She nervously tucked her hair behind her ear and smoothed the front of her new suit as she followed Mrs. Landers' sturdy form across a wide expanse of carpet toward a huge set of cherry double doors.

Mrs. Landers flung open the doors and Sandy caught sight of Marco standing behind his desk.

Her heart began to beat out a military tattoo. In daylight he seemed taller, darker, more imposing. The pinpoints of artificial light from the ceiling made light and shadow on the harsh beauty of his chiseled features. He was on the phone but as soon as he saw her, he excused himself and hung up. Mrs. Landers swept efficiently out of the room and closed the doors behind her.

Marco rounded the desk and in two long strides he loomed over her, menacing in his dark suit. A hurricane stirred in the gray depths of his eyes as he narrowed them to study her.

"I thought I'd lost you for good." His low voice had an edge to it. Anger and accusation.

Sandy swallowed, gulping back her pride. "I'm sorry."

"You're sorry?" He raised an eyebrow. "I'm not sure I've ever been left sitting in a restaurant all by myself. Wondering what happened to my date. But then I don't suppose I've ever been on a blind date with a total stranger before."

"You took a risk." She lifted her chin.

He nodded slowly. Appraising her. She was aware of the laser focus of his attention as his eyes grazed over her face, over the defiant tilt of her chin as she looked up at him. Over the smooth fabric of her fitted suit, her legs, their length accentuated by high-heeled shoes. He watched her silently, warily.

He watched her as if she might explode at any second.

Something that seemed like a definite possibility.

"I remembered an important meeting I had to attend." Her voice sounded so meek and quiet that it threatened to undermine her businesswoman charade.

"At midnight?" He raised his eyebrows, incredulous. Daring her to make him believe.

"A phone meeting. With clients in Hong Kong." The honest truth, dressed up a little for show. She raised her chin a little higher.

"Huh." Marco put his hands on his hips and cocked his head. "And you couldn't spare thirty seconds to say goodbye?"

"I'm sorry." She shrugged, holding up her hands.

Marco let out a quick snort of laughter. "I guess I asked for it, laying my body on the line for a good cause. You never know who's going to win you when you put yourself up a the prize in a raffle."

So true. A stab of recrimination made her recoil

inside. For a moment Sandy wished with a soul ache that she could be someone worthy of Marco Danieli. She had a sudden impulse to turn and run for the door. Past Mrs. Landers, past the elevator operators, past the doorman, and out into the anonymous crowds on the midtown streets.

Marco hadn't mentioned her sneaker and she had a growing suspicion that he wanted revenge. Her nerves jangled with apprehension, but she couldn't let him see that. She was used to concealing her feelings, hiding her fears. To staring people down and defying them to say she was lying. She'd thought that was all behind her, but the past had a way of clanking along behind you like a ball and chain.

He moved a little closer.

She found herself testing the air, hunting with her senses for a reassuring trace of the spicy cologne he'd worn on their date.

Nothing.

No scent she could put a name to. But her senses became alive with awareness of his body. His tailored suit barely concealed the power of his hard-sprung masculinity.

Sandy's blood surged, approaching boiling point as she struggled to hold herself still. To look calm, cool and collected while inside she was anything but. Her pulse pounded in her throat. For a single second she thought he was going to take one step further forward and either knock her down or pull her into his arms. But he did neither.

Instead he turned and walked toward his desk. He bent down behind it and she heard the rustle of a plastic bag as he retrieved something.

Her sneaker.

He straightened and held the inelegant piece of footwear in both hands. Rested it on his palms like a valuable item on display to a crowd of admirers.

"Look familiar?"

Sandy gulped and nodded. Words had departed her.

"The coat check guy gave it to me. I guess he mistakenly assumed that we knew each other."

"I know. I called there to ask about it."

"Do you always bring sneakers along on a date? Or only when you're planning to run out on someone?"

Sandy involuntarily bit her lip. Marco's eyes smoldered with the simmering traces of his anger, and with what looked like amusement.

"I went to the gym before our date." Her nose was probably growing as she stood there. She'd been to the gym—oh, maybe six months before their date.

"Now that I can believe." He let his eyes drift down again over her body, claiming every inch of it with his admiring gaze. "Your physique is a work of art."

Her physique shifted uncomfortably inside the rather snug gray suit she'd hurriedly bought that morning. It did flatter her slight build. The saleslady had oohed and aahed and wished she could look so good.

"Thank you."

Marco looked down at her sneaker. It looked ridiculously small in his hands. He narrowed his eyes and tipped his head back. "I was about ready to send out teams of horsemen to all the ladies in the land and have them try on the sneaker to see if it fit. All so I could find a mysterious damsel who disappeared into the mist at the stroke of midnight."

"It was eleven-thirty."

"Was it? Huh. I didn't check my watch until I noticed the chair opposite me had been empty for an unnaturally long period of time."

He tossed the sneaker up into the air and caught it. He studied it with exaggerated interest. "They don't make glass slippers like they used to."

Sandy couldn't suppress a laugh. A nervous giggle.

"Here." Marco tossed the sneaker toward her. She quickly threw her hands up and caught it. "It's yours. You can put it on and run for the hills if you want."

"Thanks." She hid the sneaker behind her back. Bit her lip. She wanted to beg his forgiveness, but she didn't deserve it.

Marco watched her. He stood with one hip slightly lower than the other, his head cocked slightly to the side, a challenging stance. Challenging her to turn and leave.

Challenging her to stay.

"You're not running. Does that mean I should throw caution to the dogs again and ask you out?"

A delicious shiver of apprehension and anticipation made Sandy clutch the sneaker more tightly behind her back. She lifted her chin a little. "If you like living on the edge."

Marco raised an eyebrow. "Apparently I'm quite the thrill seeker. Are you free tonight?"

"Yes." No other answer was possible.

Again she'd have to leave to be at her job at midnight.

And she have to keep that from him so he didn't know she was his employee.

But she didn't care. Whatever happened, it would

be worth it.

"I'll pick you up. Where are you staying?"

She froze. She couldn't let him find out where she lived. Then he'd know she wasn't who she pretended to be. "Uh, it's far. How about we meet here in the lobby?" It was all she could come up with quickly.

"The lobby it is, then. At eight." He narrowed his eyes again. "You will show up." It wasn't a question but a command.

"We'll be going to a party. Cocktail attire."

He shot a smoky glance at her that seemed to strip away her suit and her haughty demeanor. The heat of his gaze made her uncomfortably aware of the steady bump, bump, bump of her heart. A heart not likely to escape unscathed from this adventure.

He strode across the room and flung open the double doors for her to exit. No goodbye. She flew out of his office and across the lobby, her heels silent on the carpet. Mrs. Landers looked up from her work and stared curiously.

Sandy contemplated saying a polite goodbye to her but wasn't sure she had enough control of her vocal chords to do anything other than croak like a frog.

At 8:00 p.m. sharp she found herself click-clicking along the lamp-lit midtown sidewalk toward the bronzed doors of the building that housed Danieli's offices. Head down, she moved resolutely toward the revolving doors, worried her courage might fail her if she didn't keep moving as fast as she could.

As she emerged from the doors into the dimly lit lobby, the sight of a tall, male silhouette made her adrenaline spike.

"Hello, Alexandra." Marco's smoky eyes twinkled

with amusement.

"Hello, Marco."

"Shall we pretend we're on a regular date and kiss hello?"

"If you like." Her heart stuttered as he leaned toward her.

He pressed a quick kiss on her cheek. His skin was freshly shaven, his lips soft and warm. For an instant the city disappeared, the growl of engines and the whine of sirens blurred into silence as she was conscious only of his lips on her cheekbone.

Then he stepped back and the droning cacophony assaulted her ears again.

He pulled her by the hand out to the edge of the sidewalk and hailed a cab, then helped her in. As he settled into the seat beside her, he turned his head and looked at her deliberately.

"You look lovely."

"Thank you." A thrill of pride warmed her. She felt pretty. In a silver dress, pale smoky chiffon embroidered with silver thread and tiny bugle beads that appeared to have been stitched on by a million fairy fingers.

Thirty-nine dollars at a closeout in the garment district. As he looked at her in unabashed adoration, the expense was more than worth it.

She kept her eyes pointed straight ahead while the cab bumped and jiggled its way through the traffic.

"We're going to Tavern on the Green, in the park. It's a friend's tenth wedding anniversary. Dinner and dancing."

The soles of her feet tingled at the thought of dancing again with Marco. Memories of their dance in the jazz club had sneaked into her sleeping and waking dreams. Thoughts of moving with him again stirred her body into a restlessness she had to struggle to contain.

And maybe Marco was feeling the same way as he shifted slightly in the tight space of the cab.

"Are you going to be in town long?" he asked after a pause.

"Not much longer."

Marco nodded. He understood their date was not the next step on the road to a romantic commitment. An evening of pleasure, a few hours of joy. So what if they were to be followed by weeks or months of recrimination and longing? They had tonight.

Sandy plastered a smile on her face as Marco led her into the room full of elegantly dressed, laughing, talking people. Men and women greeted him enthusiastically and he introduced her to all of them. This is Alexandra—no qualifying descriptors: friend, associate, girlfriend.

Marco didn't leave her side, though several people tried to draw him into conversation. He kept his arm firmly on her elbow or around her waist, as if he expected her to suddenly vanish if he let go.

As one of New York's most eligible bachelors, Marco had women swarming around him and Sandy began to feel like a talisman he was using to ward them off.

"You're very popular," she teased as a pretty redhead her own age tried to attract Marco's attention with a daring witticism and racy décolletage.

"For all the wrong reasons. These women don't see anything but a decent-looking mug and a bulging wallet. They don't care a hoot about the real Marco."

"How do you know I do?"

"I don't. But oddly I don't seem to care."

He didn't care if she was using him. And she was. Not because she wanted to hurt him. But because she couldn't bear to let him hurt her. And that was what would happen if she dared to hope for more than a few brief hours of pleasure. A twinge of remorse twisted her gut. If he knew who "Alexandra" truly was—where she came from and what she'd seen— he'd run a mile. His company prided itself on avoiding scandal.

But he didn't have to know, not tonight, and after tonight she'd call a halt to this charade before it got any further out of hand.

"Your mug isn't too hard on the eyes." She used the excuse of her comment to rest her eyes on his face for a moment. To take in the chiseled edges of his cheekbones, the prominent ridge and flaring nostrils of his nose, the smoky depths of his eyes, which danced with amusement as she surveyed him.

And last of all his mouth. Wide, sensual, curving slightly into a smile as he returned her appraisal with one of his own.

"Shall we dance?" Without waiting for an answer, he took her hand and led her through the throng toward the dance floor.

A string quartet played old-fashioned music that, not surprisingly, was keeping the dance floor fairly empty. Marco held her in the classic dance position and led her in the beginnings of a waltz.

The graceful movements of the dance suited their elegant evening attire. As they glided across the polished wood she felt like they might be a prince and princess dancing at a grand ball.

Not a successful tycoon dancing with his lowliest employee.

Perhaps not quite the lowliest. The people who cleaned the buildings, like Conchita, probably got paid less than she did. But they were unionized and couldn't be fired as easily.

Fired. She was playing with fire.

If she pushed this game too far, she'd end up out of a job and back out on the streets. Would it be worth it then?

Marco whirled her around, pulled her close for an instant, then dipped her slightly. The sudden movement made her catch her breath, then smile as they settled back into the steady rhythm of the waltz.

"Where did you learn to dance?" she asked, as he pulled her close, whirling her into another turn.

"I took a class. My ex-wife made me. Back when she thought I might amount to something." His eyes narrowed.

Sandy's heart squeezed. She knew about his ex-wife from the phone conversation, but he'd never mentioned her face-to-face. "I'm in her debt," she murmured.

"It would have been our tenth anniversary this year." His eyes were fixed on her, two steel gray beams that defied her to pretend she wasn't his late-night caller. Somehow, even in her disguise, she couldn't admit to being the wanton temptress of his early-morning hours.

"Does that make you sad?"

"Hell no. I'm glad she showed her true colors. Let me know I'm better off without her."

A lock of unnaturally straight hair whirled in front of Sandy's face as he spun her around and caught her.

Marco's "waltz" moves were getting more risqué and energetic.

Sandy's fingertips tingled as they itched to touch Marco in ways more intimate than the dance allowed.

"Do you think you'll ever marry again?"

"I doubt it."

"You seem to have plenty of willing candidates."

"Don't think I haven't put some of those candidates to the test." His eyes shone with humor.

"But they always fail?"

"Sooner or later."

Again he twirled her and her hair blinded her for a moment. Sooner or later she'd fail him, too. But not just yet.

She leaned in close, absorbing the heat that radiated from his body as they danced. "Shall we go outside for a minute?"

Marco raised an eyebrow and put his arm protectively around her shoulder as he led her to one of the French windows leading outdoors.

It was a glorious warm night, the darkness illuminated by white paper lanterns. Small groups of people stood outside, talking in hushed tones, and the sweet strains of the music followed them as they crossed the patio to a secluded spot beside a tree.

Behind the tree.

She and Marco crowded into the tight space behind a broad-trunked chestnut. She knew what they both wanted.

To touch, to hold.

To kiss.

His lips were on hers in a flash, enveloping her mouth in an urgent kiss. Her fingers rose to his face, feeling the hard lines of his jaw, winding into his hair.

His tongue penetrated her mouth, probing and licking in a dance with her own eager tongue. Her pulse hammered a rhythm more insistent than the soft music of the waltz that danced across the garden toward them. Her hips lifted toward him. Her body yearned for him, longing to take the kiss further. To shed their clothes and dance skin to skin.

She slipped a hand down over the smooth fabric of his jacket and slid it underneath. Her fingers clawed at the cotton of his shirt, scratching at the fabric, groping for the hard muscle beneath it.

Marco moaned and shifted as their kiss deepened. His hands reached lower, cupping her buttocks and lifting her, pulling her up against him.

His arousal strained against the crisp fabric of his pants. He wanted her, and he didn't care if she knew it.

Her breasts stirred under the gauzy fabric of her dress. Deep in her belly she felt a thickening of her own, a warming of the darkest, most secret places inside her that ached to be explored by this man.

She was a woman. She had desires—feelings, thoughts, fantasies. Her body found its own release in dreams.

She wanted to join with this man and find their release together.

A shudder of longing pressed her hard against him. His nose tickled her skin as he kissed her neck with soft butterfly kisses that made her heart flutter.

One of his hands now moved languorously up the front of her chest. It teased the thin silver fabric of her dress and caressed her skin through the delicate material. His fingertips rested lightly on the tip of her nipple, which strained against the fabric, craving his touch.

Sandy jumped when the clang of a spoon on a glass summoned the guests inside for dinner. She'd all but forgotten the party. She'd been lost in a private world with Marco.

"I guess we'd better go in," he said softly.

Sandy smiled. "Is my lipstick all over my face?"

"What lipstick?" Marco winked at her. "You look gorgeous."

He led her to her seat at the head table, where she and Marco were seated next to the couple celebrating their anniversary.

"Hey, Marco," said their host Dave, a big jovial-looking man in his mid-thirties with a brown beard and a colorful cummerbund strained by an ample belly. "How come you didn't tell us you have a new lady?"

Marco smiled politely and said, "Alexandra and I are recent acquaintances."

"Oh yeah? And you were just outside to check on the phase of the moon?"

Sandy bit her lip as her face heated. Then she threw her shoulders back and picked up her glass, trying to act nonchalant.

"Leave Marco alone," said his wife with a smile. She was beautiful, blonde and elegant, and looked to be a few years older than her husband.

"I can rib this guy because we go way back," continued Dave, loudly. "I'm one of the few people who knew Marco when he was still tinkering with car stereos. Easy to forget that now you're one of the richest people in the Northern Hemisphere."

"Lucky thing I've got you around to remind me."

"I still don't know how he did it," said Dave to

Sandy. "I've busted my ass in commercial real estate for fifteen years and I don't have a fraction of the dough this guy does."

"It's called genius." Marco winked at Sandy.

"The hell it is. Car stereos were around before you were born."

"Car stereos are only a part of my business. My reach extends to the stars." Marco looked at Sandy and narrowed his eyes. She gulped and reached for her glass, for any distraction.

The way Marco surveyed her curiously, she was suddenly glad of the people pressed around them, preventing intimacy. Keeping her true identity safe.

Dinner hummed along, the conversation—led by the ebullient Dave—straying to politics, religion, and all the other things you weren't supposed to talk about. Voices were raised and much wine drunk. Marco talked frankly and easily with the other guests. Sandy mostly watched the conversation, chiming in when summoned for comment.

She knew more about Marco now and liked him more than ever.

Time was wasting and she didn't have all that much left. This time she'd stowed her bag in the janitor's closet inside the office building. Conchita had given her a key, but she had to hope no one would see her going inside—in her finery—to retrieve it. And she still needed time to change before her shift began. The last thing she needed were probing questions about where she'd been and with whom. Especially since her supervisor seemed to have it in for her.

At last they rose from the table and people flocked to the dance floor. It was past eleven, and Sandy was already racking her brain for a way to make her exit.

"You're not leaving tonight until I get your phone number," whispered Marco in her ear. His hand slipped around her waist, pulling her close. Clouded eyes searched her face. A little frisson of fear danced over her skin.

"I can't give out that number." She turned her head away slightly. She didn't have a cell phone. No need of one when she was either at home or on the phone at work. And she didn't want him to be able to find out where she lived—which he could if he had her home phone number.

"Even to me?" He lowered his lips to her ear. "You know my views on everything under the moon, thanks to Dave, and you can't trust me with your phone number?"

"I'm sorry." She turned to him.

His face was clouded with suspicion. "Are you a spy or something?"

"No. Nothing like that. Please stop asking me."

Marco said nothing. He took her hand and pulled her rather roughly toward the dance floor. The band was playing a fast number, and he whirled them both into it. He pulled her this way and that, spinning and dipping her so fast she was a rag doll in his hands.

He was mad.

No doubt he felt used and he didn't like it.

But she still had to leave. And not just because she had to work. If she stayed any longer, she'd lose the will to maintain her charade. The deceit was gnawing at her, sharp fingers of accusation prodding her ribs from the inside.

If she didn't get away now, she'd have no choice but to bare her soul to him, to tell him her secrets.

And then she'd see his handsome face darken with distaste. A sour end to their liaison that would leave a bitter taste in both their mouths.

Mystery never disappoints.

"I have to go to the ladies' room," she whispered in his ear when the band paused between songs.

"This time I'm coming with you." His voice was gruff. He didn't trust her.

"You can't."

"The hell I can't."

He followed her across the floor as she pushed her way through the tipsy throng of guests.

"I'll wait right here." He planted himself outside the doorway. For the first time she was aware of his bulk. He was a big man, a little threatening in appearance when he wanted to be. His expression was suspicious, wary, daring her to try to pull something on him.

For a moment she considered actually coming back out of the bathroom and explaining that she had to go but that she'd call him soon.

But it would be a lie. She couldn't call him again.

From now on she'd confine herself to admiring him from afar. Enjoying his company in her dreams.

And when she saw the bathroom had an emergency exit door leading right to the outside, she knew it was a sign. With expert ease she disabled the window alarm and slipped out into the enveloping darkness of the park.

This time he wasn't going to stand around like a chump. When Alexandra didn't emerge from the bathroom after two minutes, Marco pushed the door open. He didn't care if he surprised some broad reglueing her eyelashes.

He pushed past the empty stalls and saw the exit door.

"Damn her!"

He shoved out through the exit door into the unlit blackness of the night.

She couldn't have gone far.

It had started to rain and the pattering of raindrops muffled any sounds that might betray which way she'd gone.

A single streetlight illuminated a bench on the far side of a grove of trees, and for a split second he thought he saw a shadow jump off to the side of his vision.

He took off toward the shadow at full speed. It moved again, ducking behind a tree. As he pulled closer he saw a female form crouch down, remove her shoes, then take off in the direction away from the light.

"Alexandra!"

She didn't pause. She was fast, darting around trees and over the rock outcroppings, running in her bare feet.

Raindrops blurred Marco's vision as he ran after her, gaining on her with his longer stride.

As she approached a wide expanse of grass, he put on a burst of speed. He pelted across the grass until he managed to throw out an arm and tackle her to the ground.

He fell heavily on top of her, and she cried out as they hit the wet grass together.

He rolled her over onto her back. Her eyes were wide with terror, her wet hair clung to her skin, and her mouth opened as if to scream.

Marco stopped and stared down at her. *What the hell was he doing?*

If she wanted to go, why didn't he let her? What was he doing crashing through the park like a caveman, wrestling a woman to the ground in a show of his superior force?

He sat back on his heels and looked at her.

What was this woman doing to him?

She sat up, pushing wet hair out of her face. For a split second she looked ready to leap up and run, then her shoulders slumped in resignation.

"I'm sorry," she said.

"I'm sorry, too. I shouldn't have jumped you like that."

They looked at each other as the raindrops poured softly over them. The smell of wet grass and drenched earth rose around them. Sandy's dress clung wetly to the alluring lines of her slender body. Her nipples stood out against the silvery cloth.

Her hair hung in curly tendrils that framed her face and made her look like a wood nymph—a mystical creature visiting from another realm to torment him with her unattainable beauty.

He reached toward her and rested his hand on her arm. He half expected her to evaporate into the darkness, as she'd tried to do by running away. His fingers touched warm flesh. A living, breathing woman, panting slightly with the exertion of her attempted escape.

He pulled her toward him, and she melted into his arms. Their lips met in a hot and breathless kiss. Hungry and desperate with unfulfilled longing, they let their mouths roamed over each other. Marco's hands squeezed and held her body through the sodden fabric of her dress, pulling her close.

Her delicate fingers slid over the skin of his face, up into his wet hair. She clung to him, kissing him hard, wanting him as much as he wanted her.

Then she pulled away.

Her face was taut, and desire warred with fear in her eyes.

"I have to go."

"I know you do."

He watched her hesitate. If she was determined to leave him, to disappear without giving him a way to contact her, then he'd let her go.

"Will you see me again?" His voice sounded strange to him. He was used to making demands, not begging acquiescence.

"Perhaps."

And with that tentative word still hovering in the air between them, she took off again across the broad, flat expanse of grass that led back toward the lights of the Tavern and Central Park West.

Marco rubbed a hand over his wet face.

There was no question of going back to the party drenched and disheveled, so he set out for home. His body tormented with longing, he strode across the darkened oasis of the park, his only companions the night creatures rustling in the undergrowth around him.

4

Conchita was waiting in the janitor's closet when Sandy opened the door, panting from her run across Chelsea. Sandy managed to suppress a cry of alarm, and the tiny woman pulled her in behind the closed door and tut-tutted over her drenched appearance. "What happened?"

"It was wonderful." She admitted. "He took me to a party."

A big grin crossed Conchita's wrinkled face. "See? I told you he'd make you happy."

Sanda smiled. "He's way out of my league. He has no idea I work for him. He thinks I'm a successful businesswoman."

Conchita's expression grew serious. "One day you will be."

"Not if Miss Mean upstairs has anything to say about it." She was shrugging out of her dress and into her work clothes. "I don't know why she hates me so much. If I'm not up there in four minutes I'll lose another five dollars."

"She's jealous because you're young and beautiful." Conchita pinched her cheek. "I'm jealous, too." She released one of her oddly cackling laughs. "But it makes me happy to live through you."

"I always wondered what the fairy godmother got out of it," said Sandy with a wink. She shoved her feet into her sneakers. "I'll tell you more later when my wicked stepmother takes her coffee break." She knew Conchita would want all the details—even their kiss and her failed escape attempt. She scraped her hair back into a ponytail and kissed Conchita's velvety cheek. "None of it would be happening without you."

She shoved her damp dress into her bag and scrambled for the bathroom to remove the blue contacts. Scrubbed free of her ruined makeup, her face looked younger and plainer. Marco would walk right past her if he saw her now. Which should be a relief.

The night passed quickly as she made her phone calls with one part of her brain while the other part danced with Marco in the park. At 8:00 a.m. she logged off her computer, slung her bag over her shoulder, and headed out.

She was tired but her body still hummed with adrenaline from the dance, the chase, their last kiss. Every time she thought of Marco, a fresh jolt of nervous energy made her heart trip. She could hardly wait to be safe in the privacy of her apartment, to relive their night together and savor it again in her dreams.

The elevator was original to the building, complete with heavy gates that had to be lugged open and closed before it would go anywhere. She slammed the gates shut and pushed the down button, bracing herself as the elevator lurched into its downward journey. But instead of descending wearily to the ground floor as usual, the elevator jerked to a stop on the second floor and the gates creaked open.

When she saw who stepped in, her blood froze.

Marco.

She held her breath as he spoke.

"Why the delay in shipping the new components?" He spoke to an older man she didn't recognize.

Her brain was barely able to function as her blood pounded between her ears. Marco's attention was fixed on the other man, and she shrunk into the corner, stealing glances at him out of the corner of her eye.

"The new security requirements are slowing down production," his companion muttered as he pulled the gates shut.

Marco moved further into the elevator, leaning casually against the wall. She'd last seen him in the darkened park, hair dripping into his face, fire burning in his eyes. This morning he looked calm, rested, polished. "We'll just have to work around the security issues. We can't afford to jeopardize this contract."

Sandy willed herself to remain calm while her heart thundered so loudly he could probably hear it. Her throat grew so tight she could barely swallow. She realized she was holding her black gym bag. He'd seen it, would he recognize it? Her fingers closed more tightly around the handles as her chest tightened, constricting her breathing.

Marco continued his conversation with the other man. Sandy breathed in slow, controlled sips, suppressing with great effort the urge to pant like an exhausted dog.

The elevator seemed to move so slowly that, if it weren't for the grinding of the old machinery, she might have wondered if time was literally standing still.

At last it clunked to a stop on the ground floor and relief flooded her muscles. She slunk further into the corner, waiting for the two men to exit.

And then Marco turned to her.

She felt like Cinderella after the ball, caught in rags with her pumpkin and rats scattering at her feet, as he looked directly into her eyes and gestured toward the doorway. She hesitated, thoughts barreling through her brain.

Surely he must recognize her?

But not a flicker of familiarity lit his calm, gray eyes.

"After you."

Her heart seized. He was merely waiting for her to leave first, a common courtesy.

Her mind whirling, Sandy jumped forward, striding out of the elevator ahead of them, clutching her bag.

As she pushed out onto the street, heart racing, she couldn't help but sneak a risky glance back at Marco and his companion. They were absorbed in conversation, totally uninterested in her or what she was doing.

Marco may have seen her, but he hadn't noticed her at all.

Sandy slouched through her usual daily routine. The adrenaline rush of being in the elevator with Marco had subsided to leave her sagging with misery.

It confirmed her worst fears.

As a blue-eyed fantasy creation in a fancy outfit, she was worthy of notice. As herself, plain old mousy Sandy Riley, she disappeared right into the background like fading carpet.

Why would Marco Danieli pay any attention to her? He could have any woman in the world. She should be grateful he was interested in her even as Alexandra.

Perhaps she could become Alexandra permanently, with a relaxer and regular use of her blue contact lenses?

But Alexandra was a myth.

Even if she assumed the look, she still wouldn't be a confident, successful business woman. She hadn't even finished college. Even though she was already twenty-four she still had three more years to go. Not because she wasn't smart, but because she'd been busy trying to keep food on the table.

She looked over at the stack of books. All the homework she had to do before her next class. Her job paid for college, and the graveyard hours allowed her to attend any class she chose. Not many companies would employ a girl with only a GED and pay the tuition reimbursement that allowed her to go to school.

College was her ticket to a better life, the ladder that would take her up out of the hand-to-mouth existence she knew. Dull as it was, this job had been a godsend because of the perks that came with it. If she lost it, she might be back washing dishes in a greasy spoon, with college a distant dream. Her whole life was balanced on a precarious tightrope of dreams and desperation, and if she wanted to put it on more substantial ground, she'd better stop dreaming and start doing.

But when darkness fell again, the dreams crept back into her consciousness.

As she rode the elevator up to work at five minutes to midnight, she couldn't help but remember her last ride only inches from Marco.

She'd first seen him in that same elevator almost a year ago. Leaning languidly against the wall, the way he'd done that morning. She'd been on the day shift at the time, and her coworkers had giggled breathlessly once he'd exited the cramped space. She was far from alone in her admiration of Marco Danieli.

Since then she'd spent her days hungry for a glimpse of him. Since she moved to nights she almost never saw him. Just the occasional glimpse if she hung around for some overtime. A cat may look at a king, right? But apparently that wasn't enough for her.

Maybe she was no different from her mother, an uneducated girl from Santo Domingo who craved excitement and attention, and didn't want the responsibility of a child. Maybe she was no different from her father who wanted easy money and wasn't willing to do an honest day's work for it.

Maybe she was cursed by her DNA to want more than she should have. And to seek it by dishonest means.

Maybe she should just accept her base nature and stop pretending she might be able to live like a normal person. Like someone who has a job because she's qualified for it. Like someone who owns a home because she earned it.

Now that she was alone, she couldn't blame her problems on anyone else. She was her own worst enemy.

And she felt that accusation never more strongly than at 2:20 a.m., when she could no longer suppress the urge to dial Marco's number. He couldn't see hers because she was able to block it from her station at work.

He picked up on the second ring.

"Hello." His voice was husky with sleep. She'd disturbed his dreams, and she found herself hoping she was in them.

"Marco."

"It's you again."

"Yes." She heard rustling as Marco turned in his bed. She pictured him lying on his back, the covers pushed down around his waist. "I've been thinking about you."

"The thinking is mutual."

Marco had taken to sleeping naked, hoping his sleep would be disturbed again. Since her last call his dreams had been more intense, more vivid. More sexual.

And another date with the beautiful Alexandra hadn't helped to keep his libido in check either.

Marco considered himself to be a man of the mind, cerebral, but now his body clamored for attention. He shifted again in bed. Suddenly warm, he pushed the sheets down past his hips. Already he was hard and excited.

Too much stimulation and no release.

"Will you do something for me, Marco?"

"If I can."

"Will you move over a little and make room for me?"

Marco felt a smile creep across his face.

"All right." He shifted on the bed. There was enough room for a crowd in his king-sized bed, but it excited him to move to the side a little, to shift himself onto the cool sheet and leave a spot of warmth for his spectral lover to lay down on.

"Thank you, Marco, it's good to settle in next to you. You're warm."

"It's a hot night."

"I hope me being right next to you won't make you sweat."

He already sensed a prick of perspiration as his body responded to the suggestion in her voice. He was tempted to go turn the air-conditioning up, but he didn't want to move from the embrace of his imaginary lover and break her spell.

"Do you enjoy it when I run my fingers along the inside of your thighs like this?" The nerve endings in Marco's skin tingled as his brain supplied the sensation.

"I do." He was surprised when his voice emerged as a growl.

"Do you like it when my tongue traces a long line from your throat, down over your chest and belly, all the way to the very tip…"

She paused. His erection sprang to attention.

"Uh-huh," he managed.

"Good. I want you to know I'm there with you. I've been lonely, Marco."

"Me too." The admission felt odd. Something stirred in his gut, and he rubbed a hand over his face. He'd denied being lonely when she last called. Afterward he'd wondered why. Lying was the one behavior he despised above all others.

Her silken voice slipped into his ear. "I thought you didn't get lonely."

"I have feelings. I just have trouble admitting

them."

"I guess we all do. We don't want to let other people know we're vulnerable. It's not easy to look someone in the face and tell them you need them."

I need you.

He remembered her saying the words the last time she'd called. More than once. His own need had echoed through his body even as he denied it.

The blinds were cracked open and a shaft of moonlight shone into his bedroom, illuminating the rumpled empty sheets beside him. Marco closed his eyes. His whole body ached with need.

He'd been alone for so long. Sure, he had people around him. He had a business to run and an unending supply of pretty girls to accompany him to all the functions that went along with it. But when the party was over, he went home alone.

Lately going home alone didn't seem like the easy way out. Since he met Alexandra, he knew he wanted her in his arms. In his bed.

Was it because he couldn't have her?

"I need you, Marco."

"I need you, too."

The admission that could take place only in faceless darkness.

"I want you here." Marco mouth released the words unbidden, and he shook his head that he could only manage monosyllables. What he was feeling didn't fit neatly into words.

"I am here." Her voice was smooth as velvet, seductive, taunting.

"No, I want to hold you." He wasn't content with dreams, wisps of fantasy that wound around him, ensnaring him. He clenched his fist, his body taut with longing. "Will you come to me?"

"Yes." The word shot into his ear like a forced confession.

"You will?" He sat up in bed. He hadn't expected her to agree. He'd expected more teasing and taunting.

"I will." Her voice was barely more than a whisper.

"Tomorrow night. Do you know where I live?" Perhaps she knew everything about him. His enchantress certainly had magical powers.

"No."

"It's 135 Fifth Avenue. Near the Flatiron building. I'm on the top floor and the elevator button says *penthouse.*"

"What time?" Her voice was so quiet he could hardly hear it. She sounded afraid. And maybe she should be. She'd wakened a sleeping giant.

"Nine o'clock." After dark. The time for dreams and fantasies to come alive.

"I'll come."

"I know you will." If believing her would make it happen, then he could believe.

The dial tone tickled his ear, but he was reluctant to hang up. He wanted to keep that electronic connection alive—a thread of hope to hang on to until tomorrow night.

He lay back down on the sheets, still aroused, hard, his muscles tight. Every inch of his body howled with need, calling for the woman it craved. The cold moonlight danced over his tormented flesh with silvery fingers of light.

Mocking him.

5

Sandy stepped into the elevator and hit the button that said *penthouse*. Her heart pounded like the jackhammer doing emergency night work out in the street. Marco had buzzed her into the building, and she wondered if he could see her on a camera. She'd thought about coming as her everyday self.

Then she'd thought better of it.

She wanted tonight to be perfect. She needed it to be the culmination of all her dreams about Marco, the night they all came true.

She knew he liked her as Alexandra. She knew that as herself she was invisible to him. Why take a chance and ruin everything? Once again she'd put in the blue contacts, arranged her hair in a shiny fall around her shoulders, and dressed in a sleek black dress and high heeled sandals that she'd found among the clearance racks.

After tonight she'd vowed she would pull herself together, buckle down to her work and school, and leave Marco alone. She'd never intended for things to come this far. She'd never intended to lead him down a garden path...to where? There was no happy ending to be had here.

She wasn't someone Marco could love. Or even

like. What would he think if he knew she'd spent six months in juvenile detention for fraud? If he knew she'd been the bookkeeper for her dad's numbers racket?

She told herself that at the time she had no choice, but the prosecutor's office hadn't agreed. Her life was what it was, but that didn't stop her from wanting to pretend, just for a little while, that things were different.

The art deco era elevator moved slowly, mechanically grinding its way upward through a building that didn't have more than six floors, according to the buttons. If it became stuck, that would be a sign.

She was always looking for signs. She supposed that was common in people who didn't feel they were in control. Of their lives. Of their destinies. Of their bodies.

Her body had gotten out of control, all right. Or it had taken over control from her mind. Harmless girlish fantasies had become a woman's desires— intense needs that couldn't be denied.

The elevator lurched to a stop and the doors eased open. Bright hallway light made her blink. She took a gulp of air and walked to the only door in the hall, a tall bronze one directly opposite the elevator.

Her finger trembled as she pressed it to the porcelain button. She listened for sounds on the other side of the door. Eventually she heard a click as the lock slid back. The door cracked open and revealed Marco in all his glory.

He smiled at her. Heat shone in his eyes, which sparkled as he pulled aside the door to admit her.

"Alexandra."

"Hello, Marco."

"Come in."

He turned and she followed him into the apartment. It was the first time she'd seen him out of a suit. Worn jeans hugged his muscled backside and broad thighs in a way that made her heart beat stronger. A cream-colored linen shirt was loosely tucked in, the sleeves rolled up over his powerful forearms.

Marco's bare feet padded silently across the gleaming wood floors as he led her into a loft apartment. Art deco with an eye for comfort: big soft sofas, glowing lamps, oversize paintings on the walls and heavy velvet curtains that hid the big windows.

Jazzy music wound through the air, its source invisible. She imagined an old-time Victrola rotating somewhere in a corner.

"Can I get you a drink?"

"Whatever you're having."

"I'll make you the house cocktail." He wandered over to a large kitchen filled with industrial-looking appliances. "Take a seat."

She settled into one of the leather sofas and arranged her black skirt gracefully over her knees. Marco dropped ice into two highball glasses and covered it with a succession of clear liquids. The deft movements of his hands made her remember how those long fingers and broad palms felt on her body. Heat of desire flushed her skin and she tore her eyes away, not wanting to be caught staring.

She could smell oregano, maybe a hint of cilantro. Dinner.

Sandy wasn't hungry. Not for food anyway. She glanced up again as Marco stirred their drinks with a tall stirrer, the ice cubes clinking against the glass.

He must have sensed her watching him, for he looked up and their eyes met and mutual awareness flashed between them. Sandy's body stirred under the soft fabric of her black dress. Nipples firm, her belly taut with excitement.

Marco looked down again, peeling a lemon with a sharp paring knife.

The lyrics of the song playing on the stereo seeped into her consciousness: "I love to see that evening sun go down…" *St. Louis Blues*, hymn of the wanton woman, waiting for nightfall so she can snare a lover.

The singer's voice echoed with the kind of longing Sandy was coming to know only too well.

She swallowed hard as Marco strode toward her, carrying the two glasses. His easy stride contrasted intriguingly with the raw athletic power of his body. As he stood over her and handed her a glass, she was aware of the sheer size of him. He was well over six foot and broadly built. Not a man to mess around with.

Not unless you were looking for trouble.

He eased himself down onto the leather sofa, next to her. Only a few inches separated them, and the space began to hum with possibility.

The icy glass in her hand dripped cool condensation down her wrist. She took a tiny sip. Sweet.

"Careful, it can be lethal." The low rumble of Marco's voice in her ear jolted her senses.

"What's in it?"

"A dash of everything, plus my secret ingredient."

"What's that?"

"It wouldn't be a secret if I told you." Marco took

a sip of his drink and winked at her slowly as he put it down on a side table. "But don't say I didn't warn you."

"I appreciate your concern," she teased, a thrill of desire shimmering under her skin. "I can see you're not going to try and get me drunk and take advantage of me."

"Don't be so sure." A wicked smile spread across Marco's sensuous mouth. A wisp of apprehension curled in the pit of her stomach.

What had she come here for? She craved his touch with a longing that made her reckless, but she was also afraid. Afraid he would learn too much about her. That he'd know she wasn't a glamorous seductress. That she was an impostor, a fake, a cheat and a liar, and not the woman he thought he wanted at all.

She looked down at the glass sweating in her hand. She could feel his gaze burning through her black dress, scorching the skin beneath. Her nipples strained against the thin fabric and she knew he saw it. She set her glass on the table and awkwardly wiped her wet hand against the fingers of her other hand, wondering what to say or do.

A storm had gathered in his eyes. The expression on his face was strange, unreadable. A little whirlwind of emotion gathered in the space between them, as their bodies stirred with awareness of each other.

Marco's hand touched her thigh, slid over it, heating her skin through the fabric of her dress. He lowered his head to her shoulder and settled his face in the crook of her neck, his lips claiming the sensitive flesh of her pulse point.

Her eyes closed and she gave herself over to the

sensation. Her body strained toward his and her arms closed around him, pulling him to her. Marco lifted her up onto the sofa and she leaned into him, kneeling on the leather as his hands roved over her agonizingly aroused body.

Her mouth sought his and their lips came together with a punishing jolt of electrical energy. Her tongue flew into his mouth and met his as their kiss deepened.

She dragged her fingers down over his body, clutching at handfuls of his soft linen shirt and the hard muscle beneath. His fingertips pressed into the skin of her back and roved down past her hips to caress the curve of her buttocks.

The masculine scent of Marco, a tang of male sweat and a hint of musky cologne, overwhelmed her senses as she buried her face against him. The roughness of his skin aroused her as she gently scratched his face with her fingertips, feeling him, cherishing their mutual touch.

She pushed her body up against his as his broad hands roamed over her thighs, shucking her dress up around her waist and exploring the delicate satin of her panties.

"You're wet." His guttural gasp made her tremble. With desire, with fear. Fear of the power of her uncontrollable longings. Every nerve in her body strained for him, her fingers pressed into his back, grabbing at him, testing him, chastising him for wanting her as much as she wanted him.

The raw juices of her sexuality soaked the silky fabric as Marco pushed against her swollen flesh with his fingertips, teasing and taunting her with his touch.

Her breasts strained against the satin of her bra,

craving his touch, and she rubbed herself against him, shameless with want.

Her trembling fingertips tugged at the buttons on the front of his shirt, half ripping at them, wanting to bare his skin and rub herself against it. The buttons undone, she shoved it down over his shoulders, baring the broad expanse of his muscled chest.

Marco tugged his wrists free of his shirtsleeves and settled his hands on her shoulders. Their eyes met and passion burned darkly beneath his hooded lids.

Marco's lips were slightly parted—in anticipation of another kiss?—as he slowly lowered the strap of her dress and the bra strap pinned to it. Sandy shuddered slightly as he bared the flesh of her breast, revealing a tight nipple, his eyes fixed on his task.

Slowly he pushed down the other bra cup, letting bra and dress settle around her waist as his fingers roamed over the hypersensitive flesh of her nipples.

A low moan escaped Sandy's mouth as he lowered his face to her breast and sucked gently, eyes closed. The primal sensuality of the gesture—a man worshipping a woman's body—shocked and intrigued her. Her mind whirled with confusion at the deepening intensity of her feelings, both physical and emotional, as this beautiful man touched and enjoyed her.

As his tongue flicked across her chest and licked her other nipple as if she were a delicious ice cream, she buried her fingers in his hair, moaning her pleasure. Gently he pushed her back onto the sofa, the warm leather embracing her as she settled into it.

Marco lowered himself along with her, his hot mouth leaving a burning trail as he crouched over her. He pulled the rest of her dress and bra down over her legs, leaving her dressed in nothing but her flimsy panties and strappy black high-heeled sandals.

Marco groaned as his eyes roamed over her. His big hands settled on the warm skin of her waist, circling it as he laid hot deep kisses on her belly. Under the skin, her insides quivered as her deepest, most female places responded to his call.

His teeth teased around the hem of her panties, pulling at them. She could hear his breathing becoming labored as he struggled with the intensity of his arousal. His fingertips joined in the struggle, tugging at the silky fabric, easing it over the curve of her buttocks and down past her toes.

She was naked.

Suddenly Marco pulled her up, raising her to her feet. She stood uncertainly on the floor in her high-heeled shoes. Skeins of jazzy music danced around her, clothing her in its mellow tones as Marco quickly unbuckled his belt and shoved down his jeans until he stood naked before her.

His body was magnificent.

He was heavily muscled like an athlete with naturally tan skin that shone in the soft lamplight. A thin curl of black hair rose like a trail of smoke above the hard arrow of his maleness.

His stance was casually aggressive, one shoulder and one hip a little higher than the other—a challenge.

They stood in front of each other, man and woman. She imagined the heart beating beneath his broad chest, powering his massive physique, pumping blood to all parts of his body, including one that seemed to dance in anticipation of what was to come.

Sex.

Sandy shivered a little as she contemplated the joining of her body with his.

She wanted him.

She was afraid.

Marco reached out a broad hand, settling his fingers around her waist, pulling her gently to him. She stumbled a little in her high heels, bumped against him, her breasts crushed momentarily against the hard planes of his chest.

A shudder shot through her. He settled his hands around her buttocks and squeezed gently with his fingers as he pulled her up against him.

Her thighs pressed against his. Muscle against muscle. His hardness poked her soft belly, ready to be inside her.

Marco dropped to his knees, removed her sandals, then wrapped his arms around her thighs and buried his face in her. Shifting his weight he eased her legs apart slightly and pushed his face up into the burning aroused flesh of her sex, licking and sucking.

Sandy gasped at the intensity of the physical sensation. She teetered on tiptoe, her legs barely holding her up. Marco's strong arms supported her as he undermined all her foundations with the dangerously erotic movements of his tongue.

Her hands grabbed at his hair, clinging as Marco hungrily claimed her sex with his mouth. She moaned as wave upon wave of unfamiliar and fearsome sensation built inside her.

Suddenly her knees buckled and she fell forward onto Marco as an internal eruption heaved through her. Her body was molten lava in his arms as a powerful orgasm shook her and made her cry out with shock and excitement.

Marco's firm arms held her steady. He kept a tight hold of her shuddering body as he rose up gradually, his face buried in the flesh of her belly, between her breasts, moaning in enjoyment of her arousal as he held her while waves of pleasure rocked through her.

When his face rose to meet hers, their mouths met in a kiss that shook the last of the breath from Sandy's body.

"Marco..." She didn't know what she wanted to say. That she felt more for him than she could ever have imagined? That her feelings went beyond mere physical longing? That she wanted to know him and understand him, as a man, as a person?

That she wanted to share everything with him.

Marco's eyes searched her face, and she saw wordless understanding written in his stern features. The gray depths of his eyes offered a communication that went deeper than the mind, deeper than the contact of flesh on flesh. A union of spirits, of souls.

Sandy's whole body felt like liquid evaporating into a guttering wisp of steam as Marco's gaze washed over her. Her nerves and muscles sang with a longing for a deeper union. An urgent need.

Marco circled her with his arms, picking her up as if she was no more substantial than a puff of smoke. He settled her back against the leather cushions of the sofa and leaned over her, settling his body warmly against hers.

His hardness pushed against her stomach, which jumped and shimmied in response. She wanted him inside her.

He unwrapped a condom and sheathed himself. Lowering his mouth to her throat, Marco sucked hard, claiming the burning flesh. He raised her hips with his hands and gently, slowly, opened her legs and eased into her.

Sandy pressed her face against him, letting the scent of him fill her nostrils as he slid into her wetness, stretching her and filling her with glorious sensation.

She opened her eyes for a split second and glimpsed Marco, eyes tightly closed, face taut with emotion.

Her lover.

Sandy raised her hips, pushing her body against him, gripping him with her hands and burying her fingertips in the hard muscles of his back. As their bodies moved together, she rubbed her face against his, cheekbone against cheekbone. Their chests bumped and jostled as their hips swung and gyrated together, their bodies straining to become one.

Tears ran down her cheeks. Shock at the intensity of the experience. Her inner muscles held him tight, hugging him as her arms clung to him for dear life.

Be with me always.

She'd never known this kind of closeness to anyone. She'd never felt so open, so free. Able to express the deepest need of her soul—not in words that could be misread or confused, but with her body.

She shuddered and Marco responded by clutching her still tighter, burying his face against hers and kissing her hard. Drawing her out, soothing her as he rocked her.

Something was building deep inside her. A rhythm more intense than the drumming of the jazz that still swirled in the air around them.

A rhythm that took over her body and her mind, depriving her of thought. Two hearts beating in a trance ceremony, a mutual hypnosis, an altered state in which only they existed.

The beat of her blood thundered in her head and pumped through her body as Marco pushed inside her, driving deeper and deeper into her. The rhythm grew more intense, driving, more insistent. Marco grunted softly in her ear as his thickness grew and shuddered inside her. Her muscles grabbed him, squeezing and rocking as shockwaves of pleasure knocked her senseless and they came together in a rapture of mutual abandon.

They fell into the smooth leather of the sofa, sweaty and exhausted with passion. Marco's breath rasped hot in her ear, labored with exertion.

She cracked open her eyelids and met his cloud-gray gaze. What she saw in his eyes frightened her beyond all measure. It was like looking in a mirror. A world of loneliness bridged for a few brief moments.

Tears still fell from her eyes. Remembering her eyes were blue, not even her own, she closed them and the tears fell faster.

Marco's thumb stroked her cheek, brushing her tears away. He didn't ask why she cried. He knew better than that. For all his power and his commanding position in the world, he was a lone soul. Someone who'd seen the dark side of human nature and carried its shadows with him.

And she'd cheated and used him.

She'd lied to him, with her blue eyes and her aggressively straightened hair, lied to him with her fancy clothes and her spike heels.

Lied to him that she was a woman of substance. Not a cast-off waif fit only to hover around the edges of society, keeping her distance from people as they kept their distance from her.

To be alone was her curse. She carried it with her in her blood, the legacy of the parents she'd failed and who had failed her. The legacy of pain that made her fear contact with others the way a whipped dog fears the hand of his master.

And she'd brought all that fear and pain and dangerous longing into Marco's world, to hurt him, too.

His big, warm arms closed around her, comforting her. Accepting her. For who she was.

No, for who he thought she was.

She blinked away her last tears. No more crying. She didn't deserve that kind of self-indulgence.

She opened her eyes, taking in the sight of her nakedness sprawled next to Marco's in the dim light from the amber lamps.

Their two bodies tangled together, legs and arms winding through each other carelessly. Two lovers resting easily, spent with passion. A dream she had dreamed.

"My dream lover," said Marco softly, shocking her with the echo of her thoughts. "It's good to have you in my arms."

"It's good to be in your arms," she said honestly.

"Dreams can come true."

"At least for a little while." Her voice cracked slightly. She didn't have the heart to deceive him.

"Hey," he squeezed his arms tightly around her. "What's this about a little while? I'm not letting you get away this time."

"You don't know me." She lifted her eyes to his face. Her blue eyes. "You don't know anything about me."

"That's a temporary state of affairs. I'm going to get to know all about you whether you want me to or not. Your mysteries are under siege."

His eyes sparkled with amusement. With determination. For him the raw emotion of their intense sexual encounter had quickly warmed to a natural human interest in his lover. He may have known pain and disappointment, but it hadn't broken his spirit the way it had crippled hers.

He was a strong man, dynamic, capable of taking on the world and driving it to its knees if he wanted. She'd read in the newspapers about legendary negotiations, patents claimed, lawsuits fought and won as Danieli Electronics climbed to its position as the foremost maker of audio equipment in the world.

Marco was a man to be reckoned with. A man who knew he deserved the best and expected to find it. To seek it out and claim it.

The way he now thought he would claim her.

How quickly Marco Danieli's interest in his mystery woman would wither and dissipate if he knew what a feeble and damaged person his lover really was.

"We didn't eat dinner yet." He was smiling. "Are you hungry?"

"A little." Something so prosaic as eating food seemed funny after the intense experience they'd shared.

"Don't move." Marco disentangled himself from her and eased up off the sofa. He strode across the room to the kitchen. Naked.

His body gleamed with sweat, his muscles thrown into relief by a single ceiling spotlight over the kitchen island.

He grabbed a pot holder and removed a steaming tray from the oven. He transferred food onto a large platter and poured two big glasses of water.

Sandy wondered if she should get dressed again, but oddly she was comfortable and warm lying on the sofa, watching him.

Marco strolled back to her, carrying the food, and set the platter down on the coffee table in front of the sofa.

He winked at her. "I'm not much of a cook, but I'm great at reheating stuff from Zabar's."

He settled back onto the sofa with her, as comfortable and at ease as if he were fully dressed. He offered her the plate of appetizers, and when she hesitated he picked up a pastry-wrapped morsel and held it to her lips.

"Blow."

She obeyed.

"Bite."

She nibbled at it. Crumbs scattered onto her breasts and she giggled.

"Too hot?"

She nodded, licking crumbs from her lips.

Marco blew on it again, then tasted it himself. "It's safe. Open wide."

She opened her mouth and accepted the tasty morsel. Marco watched with apparent pleasure as she chewed and swallowed. He picked up another one and ate it himself, watching her the whole time.

He didn't ask any questions. Despite his threat, he didn't prod and goad her into revealing any secrets, or telling any lies.

When they had eaten, he took her into his bed. They spent the night together as close as two people can be. Making love, kissing, holding each other. Not talking, not thinking about the past or the future or anything other than sharing what they had, right now, in each other's arms.

When Sandy awoke a little after 4:00 a.m., Marco was deeply asleep. He lay on his back, black hair rumpled against the pillow and an expression of quiet contentment softening his proud features.

Banishing all thoughts from her mind, she slipped silently out of bed and found her clothes. She put them on and tiptoed to the door, holding her shoes. The locks on the door were old and tricky to turn without making a noise, but she managed them and closed the door carefully behind her. Then she crept out to the elevator and rode down to the ground floor.

It wasn't until she ran down the dank stairs into the tunnel leading to the PATH train that it hit her.

The loss.

The hollow emptiness of being alone.

She'd betrayed him again.

She felt as if her heart had been ripped right out of her body, and there was nothing left powering her but sheer force of will. The survivor's instinct.

She passed through the turnstile and onto the waiting train. People looked at her in her flimsy dress, with her uncombed hair falling over her shoulders. She looked right back at them.

They knew what kind of woman she was. And she dared them to despise her as much as she hated herself.

6

Marco was still smarting. When he woke up and found her gone, he'd been saddened.

Not surprised, but disappointed.

Now he was pissed as hell.

Who was this dame who thought she could wind him up and get him all hot and horny and loopy over her and then vanish into the ether?

He was Marco Danieli, dammit! No one jerked him around like this. Not without paying a high price for it.

Sure, she had a pretty face, a well-put-together body. There were plenty of those out there. What the heck was so great about her?

She probably had a long roster of suckers in her contacts list she scrolled through every night, saying, "Who shall I torment now?"

Why couldn't he get her out of his mind? Why did his arms feel empty without her? Why did he ache to see her smile? Why did he want to...? Never mind what he wanted, she sure didn't care.

He'd like her to call him now. He'd give her a piece of his mind, all right.

He strode through the city, jaywalking in the traffic, pushing past the crowds. He was headed from the midtown office to the Chelsea building to meet with a supplier and he'd decided to walk so he could get some air and clear his head.

He wished he had a hangover. Then at least he'd know it would wear off sooner or later.

He shoved open the door into the Chelsea building. Not even 9:00 a.m. yet and already it was nearly 85 degrees and humid as a Florida swamp. He was sweating inside his suit and that didn't improve his disposition any.

He pushed the elevator button and waited for the agonizingly slow descent. If he spent more time in this building, he'd get this antique ripped out and replaced with a real elevator. He banged his hand on the gate as he saw the elevator moving upward.

To hell with it.

He strode toward the stairwell, sweat trickling irritatingly down his spine, and charged up the stairs, taking them two at a time, wishing he could shake the fog of anger and regret that dogged him.

He was so wrapped up in his morose thoughts and making so much noise clunking up the stairs that he didn't even notice another person in the stairwell until he saw a pair of feet at his eye level.

Pale blue sneakers.

They'd flashed past him and turned the corner by the time his momentum slowed enough to turn around.

What the…?

He could swear they were the same as the sneaker Alexandra had dropped. He'd held it in his hand. He'd spent some serious one-on-one time with that sneaker. He even remembered the way it smelled.

He was losing his mind for sure. Why would

Alexandra be here in this stairwell? He hadn't gotten a good look at the person but he knew it was a woman. Slim build, not too tall.

He thought he could remember jeans and a white T-shirt, but he couldn't even be sure about that. He didn't see the face.

But something lingered. Not a scent, not anything he could put his finger on. But something that set his nerve endings buzzing and sent adrenaline pumping to every cell in his body.

He knew whoever it was must have come from the call center on the third floor, since he knew the few employees on the two warehouse floors below it.

No harm in stopping up there and seeing who'd just left. He was the boss, right?

The light was already fading when Sandy got home. She had a pounding headache from trying to sell herself to temp agencies all afternoon. She was glad she'd boned up on computer software when she had the chance because that was the first thing they all asked about.

She couldn't go back to Danieli Electronics ever again.

If she had to quit school, then so be it, but maybe if she worked her butt off temping and found something else she could squeeze in—waitressing?— she'd scrape together enough for the tuition. She certainly didn't deserve any handouts from Danieli Electronics, not after the way she'd treated the boss.

The boss.

She pictured him again the way she'd seen him that morning, right before she left. Sleeping peacefully. Looking happy and contented.

Not any more. He'd hate her guts by now, and she well deserved it.

When he'd dashed past her on the stairwell, after she'd retrieved her stuff from her desk and handed in her notice, she'd seen the angry look on his face.

He was so blind with rage that he didn't even see her.

Which was good because she'd moronically worn the sneakers she'd left behind after their first date.

No matter. She wouldn't be going there again. There was no chance of their running into each other any more. A bitter swell of regret rose inside her and she gulped it back. Marco wasn't meant to be hers. Surely she'd convince herself of that sooner or later.

She was wearing the sneakers now, with her interview suit, as she strode along the cracked sidewalks from the PATH train to her house in Jersey City. A low-slung sports car parked on the opposite side of the street caught her attention.

God, not drug dealers again. The car still had hubcaps, which was a bad sign. If it wasn't dealers it probably would have been stripped by now. Or stolen.

She turned to head up the stoop outside her building, and a hand grabbed her ankle.

"Don't even think of running."

Instinctively she flinched away, a scream dying in her throat, as she looked right into the face of the one man she wanted to see less—and more—than any other.

Marco Danieli.

He'd been sitting on the stoop and he rose up, grasping her arm with his other hand as his eyes seared into her, taking in what he saw. Not the elegant figure in a dress and heels, but an ordinary girl with unruly hair in dull work attire.

He stared intently into her eyes. She realized with a jolt that they were no longer blue, and her breath lodged at the bottom of her lungs.

"Alexandra." His fingers dug into her upper arm, hurting her.

"It's Sandy." She didn't know what else to say.

Marco let out a snort of laughter. His smoky eyes, nearly black beneath lowered lids, looked into hers. "I know. After I recognized your shoes in the hallway, I went to the sales floor and asked them who'd just left. Then I looked up your information in the personnel files. Blue contacts?"

She nodded.

Her arm ached where he held it and she couldn't help but twist it a little. Marco looked down at his hand and no doubt realized he must be hurting her. He loosened his grip.

"Why?" A contemptuous sneer tugged at his lip.

Sandy cast her eyes down at the sidewalk, then up at Marco. "You never noticed me looking the way I usually do." She stopped and swallowed hard as the memories of preparing for that night flooded her brain. "I should never have gone on a date with you. The raffle was closed to employees but I entered anyway." She'd never lay the blame on Conchita, who would wonder where she was tonight. She'd have to find a way to contact her.

"Can we go inside?" Marco had apparently noticed the small crowd of spectators that was not exactly gathering so much as hovering, on stoops, in open windows.

Sandy shook her head. She was afraid of him,

afraid of herself.

"Why?" Confusion clouded his gaze.

She knew what he meant. *Why did you lead me on, trick me, torment me, make love to me in my bed and then leave me?*

"I don't know."

Because I worshipped you from afar. Wanted you. Knew I could never have you.

Not as myself.

"So are you saying we'd met before and I didn't look at you?" Marco shook his head, peering at her, obviously trying to puzzle it out.

Sandy gulped and nodded.

"Where?"

"In the Chelsea building. The elevator." She could still remember each and every time they'd ridden together. The times he'd looked right at her and seemed to see right through her.

"I was probably thinking about work."

"Yes."

Why should he look at her? What was so darn special about her? Nothing. That was the point. Her heart sank a little further.

"You're beautiful, you know." His voice was soft, his eyes wary.

Sandy looked down at the stoop.

"You don't need fake blue eyes and a ton of makeup." He lifted up her chin. "I like your real eye color better. It's warmer." He looked right into her eyes, claiming them with the smoky warmth of his own. "And your hair is so pretty."

Sandy shivered with a little frisson—fear and desire—the cocktail that Marco brewed in her.

He gently pushed a lock behind her ear. "If I

didn't notice you before, it wasn't because you weren't beautiful, but because I wasn't looking."

His gaze drifted over her cheekbones and came to rest on her mouth. Her lips trembled, wanting... She bit her lip again.

His eyes dropped lower, to her conservative gray suit.

"You quit your job."

"Yes."

"You shouldn't have done that."

"I had to."

"Why?" Confusion scored his brow, twisted his mouth.

Because I'm nothing but a lousy con artist and no good can come of me lingering in any part of your life.

He didn't say anything, probably so disgusted by her flaunting the rules of the contest that he couldn't even think of words.

She recoiled in shame, wanting to hide. "I have to go now." She pushed past him and shoved her key into the lock.

He grabbed her arm, and for a second she thought he was going to shove his way in with her. She prepared to try and wrestle herself away, but he dropped it.

She slipped into the hallway and closed the door quietly behind her. His eyes seared through the thickness of the door as it shut in his face. She staggered toward the stairs, boneless with despair.

Marco sat in the toll lines at the entrance to the Holland Tunnel, fingers drumming impatiently on the wheel to the full-volume cacophony of Miles Davis's "Bitches Brew."

Pounding on the window drew him from his brooding contemplation and he looked up to see Dave looming over the low-slung car.

"Turn the freakin' music down!" he said, as Marco lowered the window. Marco reduced the volume. "I never should have agreed to meet you in the city at this time of day. Now we're both stuck in traffic. What the heck are you doing in Jersey anyway? You look blacker than the tunnel."

"Yeah? I feel it."

A loud chorus of honks caused them both to turn their head to where Dave's driverless red Mercedes held up traffic.

"Freddie's?"

"Yeah. I need to get *drunk*."

"See you in a few." Dave flipped a finger at the impatient honkers as he climbed back into his car and continued on toward the line of toll booths.

Marco arrived at Frederico's on Prince Street first and was well into his second gin and tonic by the time Dave arrived.

"That grim look got anything to do with the pretty girl you brought to the party?"

Marco snorted with disgust and took another gulp of his drink.

Dave eased himself into the booth and signaled the waiter to bring him his usual. "What's she been doing?"

"Jerking me around. You know how women are."

"Guess I don't. Married ten glorious years and all that."

"Lucky bastard."

"You could get lucky, too."

"Yeah, right."

"Maybe you're looking for love in all the wrong places, my friend. Those glamour girls I see you with look good on your arm, but they're not ideal wife material. Could be you need to find someone a bit more down-to-earth."

Another raucous snort of disgust escaped Marco. He drained his drink, slammed the glass down and signaled for more. Numbness was the sensation he was going for. Oblivion.

"She's married." His voice emerged as a growl. She had to be. It was the only explanation for her cagey behavior. He'd tracked her to her home, told her he thought she was lovely just as she was—and she told him to leave, in no uncertain terms.

Dave winced.

"You tangle with her husband or something?"

"No way! You think I'd even touch a woman that I knew was married? No. I couldn't figure out why she wouldn't tell me where she lived. Wouldn't give me her number. She'd call me but I couldn't call her, you know?"

He glanced down at the wooden table. Someone had carved a heart into the wood, and the scar had blackened with time and wear. "Then I put two and two together."

"Wait a second here." Dave paused to take his drink and thank the waiter. "You're assuming she's married, but you don't know for sure, right?"

"I don't need it spelled out for me. I tracked her down, went to where she lives. She has brown eyes, not blue." He looked up at Dave's puzzled face. "She was all glammed up, in a kind of disguise when she came to meet me."

"Why?"

"Who knows? So her old man wouldn't catch her, I guess." Marco took another deep draught of his drink.

He was starting to feel its medicinal effects.

"Where'd you two disappear to that night, anyway? I looked for you to see if you wanted to come back to our place for drinks after the party, but you were gone."

"She ran off." Marco shook his head. "Slipped out through an emergency exit. And that wasn't the first time. Ran out on me on our first date, too."

Dave chuckled. "She sounds like trouble."

"You're telling me."

"So why were you messing around with her?"

"Witchcraft, man. She had me wound up like a fly in a spider web." He took another deep gulp. The icy liquid soothed the rawness of his pain.

"And from the looks of you she still does."

Marco sighed. He hadn't eaten all day and he was getting drunk fast. Suddenly Alexandra's—Sandy's—big brown eyes danced in front of his vision. Soft and sad. Haunting. He rubbed a hand over his face.

"There's something about her." He shook his head again, trying to banish the images and thoughts of her that came crowding in on him. "She'd call me at night. Wake me up."

"Seduce you?"

"Yeah." Marco couldn't help his lips curling into a smile, but he cut it short with another quick gulp of liquor.

"You've got it bad."

Marco looked down at the black heart-shaped scar crudely scratched into the table. It seemed a fitting symbol for his experience with love.

Love?

Hell, no. Couldn't be. He barely knew the woman.

Scratch that. He didn't know her *at all*.

"So why do you think she was after you?"

Marco shrugged. "Gold digger? Looking to dump hubby for someone with deeper pockets?"

"Then why would she run off?"

"Damned if I know." His thoughts were becoming a little fuzzy around the edges. "Wouldn't let me into her apartment when I showed up there, either. Made a lousy excuse about how she hadn't won her date with me fair and square. As if I'd care."

"Maybe she's afraid of you."

"She should be."

"I don't know, Marco, it doesn't add up. She's leading you on and slipping away, then coming back again...."

"Jerking me around like a puppet on a string."

"But why? That's not the way gold diggers work. They want to be your all and everything. Won't let you out of their sight until they get that rock on their finger. You know how that goes."

Marco nodded in assent, but his mind was elsewhere. He remembered how it felt to hold Sandy tight in his arms and wrap himself around her. The way their bodies had cupped together, a perfect fit. How good it was to have her in his bed. His woman.

Ouch, he was getting wasted.

He blew out a blast of air and shook his head, trying to clear the fog of lust that had descended over him. "Maybe she just wants to have a little fun on her terms."

"Marco, Marco, Marco. You just don't have good luck with the ladies, do you? It doesn't seem right that someone with your looks and cash is crying into his drink over a girl."

"Do you see any tears?"

"And a fat bastard like me has a lovely woman at home waiting for me. Speaking of which…"

"Go home."

"There's someone out there for you, Marco. Don't sweat it."

Marco sneered. "Someone out there for me? Yeah, right. Been there, done that. 'Til death do us part." He took another gulp of his drink. "I really loved Deanna, you know? I thought we'd be together forever."

"You were young. She was young. It was a mess. It's over."

"I thought I was cured of all that love stuff."

"And now you've fallen hard for this new girl."

"Yeah."

He must be drunk if he was willing to admit it out loud. Dave chuckled. Apparently he thought so, too.

"You're in no state to drive. Come with me."

"I'll walk home."

"Give me your keys."

Marco fished his keys out of his pocket and tossed them at Dave.

Dave winked at him. "You'll be okay."

"I know."

But he'd never been less sure of anything in his life.

He had her number. Literally and figuratively. He already knew she was Sandy Riley of 31 Elm Avenue, Apartment 4, Jersey City, New Jersey, telephone number…

He'd probably call and get her husband on the line. Then the husband would put it all together and Sandy would get it hard on the ass.

He didn't want that to happen to her.

Why the hell not?

Marco sighed. It was 2:00 a.m., right around the time his mystery caller had awakened him with sweet fantasies that stirred his blood.

Played him for a sucker.

But he couldn't get that lovely face out of his mind. Blue eyes or brown. The mouth that smiled so sweetly. The shapely body that moved like a dancer through his imagination.

The soft chuckle that tickled something deep down inside him.

The way she danced. And the way they'd made love together.

Heck, if a man picked up he'd hang up.

It wasn't in him to leave a stone unturned. He'd never move on until he got this resolved for good and all.

Just one question. All she had to say was yes or no.

He dialed the number and listened to it ring. Someone picked up.

"Hello?" Her voice, groggy with sleep.

"Are you married?"

She hesitated for a moment. Marco held his breath. His stomach muscles clenched, ready for a punch to the gut.

"No."

"Seeing someone?"

"No."

Her response, soft, quiet but unhesitating and resolute, swept through him on a tide of relief. He believed her.

"Then what are you playing at?"

"Marco, I'm not who you think I am…."

"No kidding."

"I'm no good. No good for you. You need to forget about me." He thought he heard a catch in her voice, right before he heard the ugly drone of the dial tone. She'd hung up on him.

But this time he wasn't left with a warm feeling of sensual arousal and the anticipation of more to come. He was left with an intense longing to corner her, take her in his arms, and kiss her until she told him what the heck was going on.

"I'm no good for you." What was this—a forties movie? He'd decide what was good for him, thanks.

Marco twisted on the bed. He was naked.

And now he was hard.

Apparently just the sound of her voice was enough to get him howling with lust. He rolled over onto his stomach and willed his erection to go down. He wasn't going to storm over there in the middle of the night and frighten the life out of her.

But he wasn't going to let her walk away.

He had an important meeting tomorrow with the president's top security adviser about voice-print security systems for the White House and the Pentagon. And the LAPD was interested in the sound activated radios they'd seen. He had to nail that deal tomorrow before the competition moved in.

But after that….

7

She had a job! It wasn't the best, but it would pay the bills. She'd be filing and pulling records in a medical office—during the day so she'd have to start taking night classes. No problem, though. Plenty of people took night classes.

Her new job didn't pay enough to cover tuition, but she'd called about working in university maintenance doing late-night cleaning. That would get her a few dollars and a tuition reduction if she did at least thirty hours a week. She wouldn't have any time left for herself, but what did she need that for?

It wasn't like she had any social life. It wasn't like she had a—

No. Don't even think about him.

As Sandy turned onto her street, she scanned for any sign of a flashy sports car. She'd probably be doing that for the rest of her life.

Nothing.

Good. No, really, it was good.

Then why did she have this unpleasant sinking feeling?

Get over it, Sandy!

Why did he have to call her? She'd hated herself for hanging up on him, but she hadn't known what else to do. Getting involved with her would be bad for his reputation. His company had highly sensitive government contracts. Employees at the top levels went through stringent security screening. She'd committed at least one sin of omission on her application form and even though juvenile records were sealed, if her name—and her father's—were linked with his.... Well, that would be bad for all concerned.

She'd lain awake all night cursing herself for letting herself get talked into this whole mess in the first place. She'd let Conchita seduce her into breaking the rules—by using a ticket she should never have won. Had she still not learned to say no? She still hadn't figured out how to explain her sudden departure to Conchita, who'd be devastated if she felt responsible for Sandy leaving her job.

She'd only hoped for one enjoyable evening to cherish as a memory. Her plan had gone awry when one date wasn't enough—for either of them. Each time she'd hurt Marco had been a stab to her own heart. He didn't deserve to be treated like that. He was a good man, kind, caring, an attentive lover...

Stop it, Sandy!

Her shoulders slumped as she saw the empty stoop. Had she truly expected him to come track her down?

She slid her key into the lock, then hesitated when she heard raised voices on the other side of the door. A man and a woman. She recognized her landlady's high-pitched voice.

"I'll have you arrested!" Mrs. Patel squawked. "You have no right!" Frightened for the frail older woman, Sandy turned the key and shoved the door open. She crashed into the hallway, prepared to defend her with force if need be.

"Sandy." Marco. He towered over both of them.

"Do you know this man?" The tiny woman stood with her hands on her hips.

"Yes," whispered Sandy.

"He would not believe you weren't here. Forced his way in! Insisted on sitting on my steps until you came back!"

Sandy looked at Marco. His storm-cloud eyes searched her face.

"I didn't like the look of him one bit. I'm not in the habit of having brutes lounging around in my hallway, laying in wait for young ladies on their way home from work."

Marco wore jeans and a black T-shirt. Without his suit he didn't come with any unspoken promise of respectability.

"And I know this young lady is not the type of girl who entertains men after hours." Her darting, birdlike eyes hopped from Marco to Sandy and back to Marco. "She lives quietly. And you...." She waggled an accusing finger at Marco. "You don't seem like the type of—"

"It's okay, Mrs. Patel. He's a friend." Sandy's voice barely rose above a whisper. She avoided Marco's eyes.

"That's all right then," said Mrs. Patel slowly. Her forehead wrinkled. "I don't mean to intrude. But I worry about you, a young girl all alone."

"Thanks, Mrs. Patel, I appreciate it."

Marco stood silently during the exchange. When Sandy signaled for him to follow her up to her apartment he nodded to her landlady and climbed the stairs behind her.

"Thanks," said Marco, after she'd closed her apartment door behind him. She immediately felt ashamed of her Spartan railroad apartment, with its cast-off furnishings. She picked up a plate with an orange peel on it that she'd left on the table and put it in the sink.

Like that would help.

The jig was up. He could see how she lived. No glamour here.

But Marco wasn't looking around her apartment. His eyes were fixed tightly on her, dark pupils searching her face, wandering over it, claiming it. Sandy's throat tightened as his eyes dropped to her neck, her collarbone. Heat surged through her, appearing no doubt as a revealing flush.

"You didn't think I'd just let you go?"

Did she? She felt ashamed of how she'd hoped he'd come after her. She'd realized that when she caught herself looking for his car, hunting for him on her street.

"You should." She swallowed hard, holding his gaze with considerable effort.

"Don't try to tell me what I should do. I can decide for myself." His eyes were blackened by unreadable emotion.

"I'm not who you think I am." The words almost choked her.

"So you keep saying. Right now I have no idea who you are, so that line of thinking is irrelevant. I just know you are…you."

Sandy wore her conservative gray interview suit, and she was grateful for the stiff fabric that concealed the way her body was trembling.

The heat was oppressive. Sandy crossed the modest space that was both kitchen and living room to shove open the dingy window and turn on the fan.

"Could I have a glass of water?" asked Marco.

"Sure." She was glad of the distraction of filling a glass with cold water from the jug she kept in the fridge. At least her hospitality was able to stretch that far.

"I'm sorry it's so hot in here."

"No problem." Marco swallowed his water in one long draught and set the glass down on the table. She couldn't help but notice the latent power in the coiled muscles of his forearms. Tan skin with a dusting of black hair.

She remembered the way his hands had felt on her body. Their touch so tender, their caress so arousing. Sweat darkened his black T-shirt in the hollow between his pectorals, and he rubbed at the spot while they watched each other in silence.

Lord, it was hot.

"Why don't we start over? I know you're Sandy Riley, you have lovely hazel eyes, and you live in an apartment in Jersey City, conveniently located for commuting to your—former—job as a sales representative at Danieli Electronics."

"I found a new job."

He nodded approval. "Good for you."

"I don't make much money."

"So? I make my own money. I'm not looking for a woman to support me." His eyes roved over her face, and a smile tugged at the corner of his mouth.

"I only have two semesters of college," she said, anxious to shatter the rest of the illusion.

"That's two more than me then."

"You're kidding."

"Nope. Didn't go. Taught myself."

"Oh." Oddly, the information soothed her. Her own lack of education made her feel insecure around those who had far more knowledge and refinement. "Like Bill Gates."

Marco laughed. "Don't let him hear you say that. But yeah." He raked his fingers through his black hair, then wiped a forearm across his brow.

"I'm sorry it's so hot."

"You don't have to keep saying that. It's hot everywhere. Can we sit down?"

"Of course. I'm a lousy hostess."

"And you can change out of your suit if you want. I won't even insist on watching."

Though I'd be more than glad to.

The unspoken addendum shone in his eyes.

Sandy was glad of the excuse to duck out of his presence, even for a minute. Her heart thudded against her ribs, perspiration trickled down her back, and her body was giving her all sorts of mixed signals that were making routine thought quite a challenge.

She closed the bedroom door quietly behind her and slipped into a light summer dress with a floral pattern. She pinned her hair up off her neck, leaving a curly strand or two loose to soften the look. Not exactly glamorous, but so far Marco wasn't complaining.

He actually seemed to like the way she looked.

That was more than a little frightening. It was one thing to attract his attention, to flirt with him, while wearing a mask. It was quite another to think she might hold his interest as herself.

The thought of him sitting on her sofa made her

pulse skitter. Now that she'd seen him naked, it was hard to look at the broad chest in the black T-shirt and not picture in detail the swell of the hard muscles beneath it.

She dabbed a touch of cologne behind each ear—why not?—and walked back into the living room.

Marco's face warmed with appreciation as he took in her breezy dress and bare feet. "You look pretty."

"Thanks." The temperature seemed to shoot up another five degrees as his smoky gaze simmered over her body, as if he could see right through the gauzy fabric of her dress.

"Come sit down." Marco motioned to the empty space on the sofa beside him. Swallowing hard, Sandy padded across the floor and eased herself into the spot. She resisted a sudden urge to fan herself with her hand.

"Now…" He leaned toward her slightly, tilting his body so he faced her head on. "I want to know why you pretended to be someone else when we met."

"It's not easy to explain."

"I don't care if it's easy or not. Don't you think I deserve an explanation?"

"Yes." Sandy bit her lip. "I guess I just wanted…to be glamorous. I've seen the photos in the magazines of all the beautiful women you go out with. I knew you didn't notice me the way I normally look. I wanted that one night to be special. I never intended it to go beyond a single date."

Marco lowered his lids. His eyes smoldered, suspicious and intrigued. "And why did you run away?"

"I had to get to work."

"And you couldn't just say, 'Hey Marco, I've got to

be at work at midnight,' and I'd have said, 'No problem, may I have your phone number so we can make plans to get together again'?"

Sandy shook her head. "Then you'd have known I wasn't a successful career woman."

"But you are. You've got a good record. I read your personnel file when I was rifling though it looking for your address."

Sandy raised an eyebrow, challenging him. "I'm a telemarketer. How many telemarketers have you dated?"

"Only one, as far as I know, but who knows how many of the other women I've dated were telemarketers in disguise." Marco winked at her.

The gesture sent a shimmer of sensation up her spine and made heat gather low in her belly.

Marco leaned toward her a little. "There's no shame in selling products for Danieli Electronics. At least I don't think so."

"Oh no, I didn't mean to imply that... But I shouldn't have entered the contest at all."

"You didn't. Your name wasn't on the list of raffle winners."

She bit her lip.

Marco placed his finger over her mouth. "No more lies." The touch of his fingertip sent an electrical tickle of sensation that stung her mouth, making her lips part slightly. Every inch of her body tingled with awareness of him.

"A friend gave me the ticket. I won't say who."

"Well, whoever your friend is, I owe her a debt of gratitude." Marco's eyes held hers, searching. "You ran away, but then you gave me my third wish anyway."

Sandy bit her lip. "I wanted to see you again."

"I liked the phone calls. They were very…provocative. At that hour you must have called me from work."

She blushed. Making sexy phone calls to the boss while on the clock had to be grounds for dismissal. Lucky thing she'd fired herself already.

"Yes." She hesitated. "I told you I wasn't someone you'd want to know."

Marco grinned. "I like you more every second. I'm picturing you sitting in one of those anonymous gray cubicles, whispering sweet nothings into the phone while I'm tying myself up in knots at the other end."

"I'm sorry."

"I'm not." His voice was a husky murmur. "I took my clothes off for you. I didn't want to lie to you after I'd told you I was naked. You made me strip. You made me crazy."

His eyes shone with amusement. And desire.

Sandy felt a curl of excitement below her belly button. Her body strained toward him even as she tried to hold it in check. Her nipples tightened beneath the light fabric of her dress, and she wondered if he could see them.

"I couldn't help it. I hadn't meant to talk to you again. To see you again. But…" She paused, not sure what to say.

"But you felt the connection between us, too." His voice rumbled low.

"Yes."

"And can you feel it now?" The thundercloud darkness of Marco's eyes hinted at a storm that neither of them would be able to control.

"Yes," she whispered, as desire and unspeakable

emotion whirled in the air around them.

Sandy leaped to her feet. "Would you like some more water?" she gasped.

A sudden burst of adrenaline propelled her across the room. Fight or flight! Too clearly she could imagine Marco's hands on her body, his lips on hers—

She held her glass under the faucet, forgetting about the iced water in the fridge. She held her hand under the water, then her wrist, letting the cool cascade flow over her pulse point. Trying to cool her blood.

It was far too hot.

She glanced back at Marco, who'd lifted the hem of his T-shirt to wipe his face with it. The gesture revealed the flat expanse of his stomach. The view was extended as he lifted his T-shirt up over his head, pulled it off and mopped at his neck and broad shoulders.

"Too hot," Sandy breathed. The sound of her own voice startled her. She'd spoken her thoughts aloud.

The sight of Marco sitting shirtless on her sofa was more than she could bear and remain sane. As she watched, he rose from the sofa and used his balled-up shirt to dry the skin of his back.

"Sorry," he said, looking at her. "This isn't too gentlemanly, but I don't want to perspire all over your furniture."

"That's okay," she choked.

"Thanks." As he took the glass from her, his fingers brushed against hers. A current of sensation shot up her arm. All the way to her nipples, which bloomed with awareness of his body.

Marco drained the glass and set it down. Then he

reached out and placed his hand on her waist. Her eyes were level with his collarbone and she saw the muscle moving above it as his hand slipped behind her back.

Softly he tugged her up against him. Her breasts bumped gently against the bare warm skin of his chest. He settled his other arm around her, enveloping her.

"God, it feels good to hold you," he murmured.

She pressed her face into his shoulder, inhaling the musky scent of hot, sweaty male. Her heart jumped. Slowly she lifted her arms and circled them around his torso.

Holding Marco felt so right.

In his arms, Sandy felt her nagging doubt surrender to the inevitability of their coming together. As they held each other, the storm built inside them. She could feel it, starting in her heart, rushing though her belly, her breasts, down to her legs and the throbbing dark space between them.

Marco lowered his mouth to kiss her. Her lips parted and welcomed his probing tongue into the warm depths. She groaned, writhing against him as shockwaves of sensation coursed through her body.

He held her tightly, stroking her back with his hands, protective. The strange comfort of being safe in his arms clashed with the passion he created in her. Heat radiated from the core of her body as blood rushed to her sex. Marco's big hands drifted down to her buttocks, cupping them and pulling her up toward him.

Crushed against the hard muscles of his torso, her breasts throbbed and tingled, wanting Marco's hands on them.

As if he read her thoughts, Marco pulled back from her a few agonizing inches and lifted his hands to her breasts, settling his palms over the nipples. He teased the hardened peaks with his thumbs, then lowered his mouth over her right breast, sucking the nipple deeply through the thin fabric of her dress.

Sandy's body bucked at the intense sensation. Her hands knitted themselves into his sweat-dampened hair as she let out a soft moan.

Obviously aroused by her abandon, Marco sucked harder, rubbing the other breast with his broad fingertips until the peak was hard as steel.

Sandy's whole body quivered with the agonizing overload of desire.

"Make love to me," she murmured.

And she meant it. Love. She wanted to make love to Marco, to have him make love to her. No apologies, no excuses. Consequences be damned.

And she couldn't wait another second.

Pulling him to her, she struggled with the button fly of his jeans, ripping the buttons from their holes with trembling fingers.

The visible evidence of his arousal made her aware of how wet she was. Marco cupped her sex with his fingers, feeling her heat through the fabric of her dress.

He groaned. He tugged at the top of her dress and pulled it down over her breasts. He paused to lower his head and lick the bare flesh of her nipples, then pushed her dress down past her waist to the floor, where it pooled around her feet. Her panties quickly joined the rumpled dress and once again she stood naked before him.

But this time she wanted to lead the dance.

She hesitated, and his eyes opened. She looked into them, licking her lips and flashing a challenge. Then she pushed him gently, shoving him toward the big armchair that stood behind him. His legs bound by his half-lowered jeans, he fell backward into the chair with a grunt.

Sandy yanked at the hem of his jeans and freed him before climbing over him, poised to mount the glistening rod that rose from the dark hair between his legs.

"Protection," moaned Marco, his face pained. "I didn't...I..."

"I have some." Sandy had prepared for her visit to his apartment. She raced into her bedroom and rifled through her things until she unearthed the small box of condoms.

Her body was screaming with the agony of her arousal as she settled herself urgently on Marco's lap, clawing at the packet with her fingertips. Marco quickly took it from her, expertly ripped it open, and sheathed himself.

Her arms wound tightly around his neck, her sex warm and wet, Sandy lowered herself slowly over Marco's member. She let out a low, guttural groan of pleasure as his hard, male flesh filled her.

Bracing her knees against the arms of the overstuffed chair, she raised and lowered her body over him, glorying in the sensation that flooded every part of her.

She sought his lips and kissed him. Her mouth roved over his, her tongue teasing and jousting. Marco's scent filled her senses as she pressed against him.

His hands covered her breasts, rubbing and

caressing as she slid up and down. His erection shuddered inside her as she moved.

She cupped Marco's face in her hands, possessing him. His eyelids were closed, the muscles of his face taut with emotion. In her hands, under her body, he gave himself over to her, trusting her.

He wanted her even after all the things she'd done wrong. He was willing to take a chance on her, to risk his body, to risk his heart. His generosity shook Sandy to the core.

Her life was shaped by fear, guided by the desire to avoid pain. Marco was braver, stronger, fearless in his pursuit of what he wanted. What he needed.

What they both needed.

His hands closed over her buttocks, pulling her to him, increasing the intensity of the rhythm. Blood rushed though her as the push and pull of their bodies mirrored the edgy tango of the dance she'd led him on.

Her breath escaped in ragged gasps as Marco moved her harder, faster, taking the lead and driving them both to the brink of heaven, the brink of madness.

Her innermost muscles squeezed around him, clutching at him, echoing the rhythm of her thundering heartbeat. Suddenly Marco gripped her. A deep moan filled her ears as their joint climax shook them like a devastating earthquake. Sandy felt herself letting go, falling into his arms, breathless and suffused with pleasure.

How could she ever walk away from him now?

8

"Don't you dare get up." Marco grabbed at Sandy's ankle as she tried to get out of bed. "You're not going anywhere without me, lady."

He was grinning. They were both relaxed and rested, enjoying the morning sun as it streamed through the blinds of the single window in Sandy's bedroom.

"I have to pee."

"Not without a security detail. There's a window in that bathroom."

"But I have no clothes on."

"That doesn't reassure me one bit."

Sandy struggled against Marco and he lunged forward and grabbed her around the waist, wrestling her down onto the bed. He flipped on top of her and pinned her, the sheer weight of him holding her firm against the mattress.

And giving him a delicious opportunity to savor the softness of her body.

"Being big has its advantages."

He watched a smile creep across her mouth, lighting up her pretty features and sparkling in her hazel eyes.

"Big muscles will get you but so far." Her eyes

narrowed, and she did something with her fingers that caused a stab of pain to spike through his gut. He flinched aside, and she almost escaped.

But not quite.

"That was a dirty trick. Didn't work though, did it?"

Sandy bit her lovely pink lip and looked up at him shyly. "Sorry."

"Where did you learn that, the Marines?"

She shook her head.

"The CIA?"

"No."

"The mob?"

"Not the mob." She actually paled a bit.

"You're so darn secretive I don't know what to make of you. I wish you'd just lay your cards on the table."

Did he? Part of him wanted to plumb her mysteries and be done with it. But part of him loved the tease, the wondering, the speculation about who she was. What she'd done that made her so afraid to let him into her life.

And there was the element of fear, too. What if her past did contain a secret that was truly devastating?

Unforgettable.

Unforgivable.

He remembered she needed to use the bathroom. He rolled off and let her go. Didn't take his eyes off her for a second as she walked gracefully across the floor, long limbed and lovely, into the tiny bathroom.

God, she was beautiful. And passionate. Sensuous and tender, a natural lover. Not experienced—that was obvious, but in no way an impediment to their mutual pleasure.

He'd slept with women who knew every trick in the book, but no amount of studying the *Kama Sutra* compared with plain old-fashioned good loving. And she'd given him plenty of that.

Marco groaned softly. He was becoming hard again. He just couldn't get enough of this woman.

She was probably climbing out the window right now wrapped in a hand towel. And he didn't even mind. If she took off again, he'd find her. Track her down and love her.

He was in deep.

Lust was the curse of man. It drove him into the arms of women he should run from. Exposed him to the claws of gold diggers, hustlers, social climbers, and those who simply wanted to sleep their way to the top.

All in the name of *love*.

Now loving was the joyous act of mating. Of joining up with a fellow human in a blissful experience of togetherness. The union of bodies, and maybe even a little nudge of souls, a brief flare of the kind of closeness he couldn't stop craving. This kind of loving was good in its own right. It was enough, and he'd learned not to expect more.

Sandy emerged from the bathroom wearing a white cotton kimono that stopped at the middle of her thighs. Her curls framed her face like a halo, and Marco struggled with a sudden urge to bury his face in their soft caress.

"I don't have any food for breakfast, except oranges."

"I could eat you."

"I won't stick to your ribs."

"Oh, yeah?" He lunged forward and tackled her around the waist, pulling her back onto the bed with him. "Maybe you will if I hold you tight enough."

Sandy chuckled. She wriggled on top of him, teasing. He was still hard. "I can tell you're a man of insatiable appetites."

He tickled her and she giggled. He nipped her ear, kissed her quickly on the cheek. "I can't get enough of you."

Their lips melded into yet another sensual kiss that made Marco's whole body sing with joy. He didn't want to get out of bed. Getting up would mean the night was over and their relationship was moving into some new and unpredictable phase.

He still hadn't managed to unveil much about the elusive Sandy.

"Why did you call yourself Alexandra Alma when we went out on our date?"

"I didn't want you to figure out I worked for you."

Marco chuckled. "I probably wouldn't have figured it out anyway. I don't memorize the employee listings."

Sandy winced. "I was sales rep of the month four months ago. I wasn't sure if that information made its way up to you."

"I'm afraid it doesn't. But wait a minute here—my sales rep of the month quit on me?" He rolled over until he was on top of her, pushing her down into the bed. Desire spiked through him as he enjoyed her lush curves under his body. "I don't think I can afford to lose you as an employee. Will you come back to work for me?"

"I don't know if that's a good idea." Her face was suddenly serious. Her hazel eyes glittered with apprehension that twisted his gut.

"Maybe you're right." Who knew how this would end? All Marco knew was he didn't want it to end. Not yet.

"Sandy, would you do something for me?" He rolled off her and stroked her gently through the thin robe. He couldn't get enough of the softness and warmth of her body. Of the way her whiskey gaze made his heart swell.

"Depends what it is."

"Well," he hesitated. Suddenly the idea seemed crazy, but he couldn't resist asking anyway. "It's my dad's sixtieth birthday this weekend. My brothers and I are going over for dinner. Will you come?"

"Oh, no, no, I couldn't possibly…." Her eyes widened with alarm.

He supposed it was a lot to ask. He was never too crazy about "meeting the folks." It implied some kind of commitment. But damn it, he wanted some kind of commitment with Sandy. He wanted to get their relationship on some kind of "normal" footing—at least for a couple of hours—to reassure himself that it wasn't all a wild and wonderful dream. And maybe if she met his family she'd see him as a person, not the boss.

"It would mean a lot to me. My dad would like it, too. He's always after me to find a nice girl and I know he'd like you." His brothers would, too. Who wouldn't?

He could see she was considering it. "It's just dinner, not a big party or anything." What on earth was going through her head? Her eyes searched his face, her lips parted, she looked away, then she looked back at him.

"Okay."

"What were you thinking?" Sandy looked at herself in the mirror as she applied lipstick. "Dinner with his family? Are you nuts?"

But being asked had touched her deeply. Gosh, dinner with the family. As if she were his girlfriend.

She swallowed hard.

Get a grip, Sandy. You're not his girlfriend. He doesn't know anything about you. That's the reason he asked you.

But that wasn't entirely true any more. He'd seen the real her, and not only did he notice her, but he couldn't keep his hands off her.

She struggled to suppress a smile. What a night...

He knew where she lived. Not the greatest of neighborhoods but not the worst either. He didn't seem at all put out by her small apartment. They must have made love on every surface in it.

She blushed at the memories. Marco was insatiable. And apparently so was she. At least when it came to him.

And that was part of the problem. This wasn't just an innocent flirtation anymore. She was falling hard for him. The way he smiled when he held her tight made her heart squeeze. His touch was so gentle, yet so assured.

And when he looked at her—really looked at her—the smoky depths of his eyes darkened with emotion; the boundaries of the known world shifted and she found herself drifting out into unknown territory, rudderless, awed and frightened by the strangeness and beauty of it all.

If she couldn't leave him alone after one date, how was she going to forget him after lying in his arms all night? After having dinner with his family?

Conchita had said she'd never speak to her again if she didn't go. Sandy had pointed out that might be a good thing.

"Trust me, chiquita. I understand these things. He's a good man."

That's exactly the problem. She couldn't say that, though. Her sweet fairy godmother knew nothing about her criminal record. "I'll go, but don't expect anything, okay?"

Marco had promised to send a car for her. He was headed to his father's house straight from the airport after a business trip. She glanced out the window and saw the long black sedan waiting outside and swallowed hard.

She knew that how she managed this evening—an ordinary family dinner—would impact her view of herself and her future. For better or worse.

Was she ready to step out into the world of ordinary, law-abiding, honest people? Was she was even ready to make friends?

She hurried downstairs and climbed into the limo, her heart pounding and her palms sweating. She wiped them anxiously on her flowered dress as she shot a nervous smile at the driver.

"Forty-seven Gloria Terrace, right?" His weathered face was scored by the deep wrinkles of a heavy smoker. And looked oddly familiar. "Hey, Sandy Riley!"

Oh, God. She recognized him, too. He was one of her father's old ex-con buddies. He flashed a grin at her and his name came to her immediately: Joey "the teeth." Named for the gold front teeth he'd once had. A surge of nausea made her clutch at the door handle.

"It is Sandy, isn't it?"

"Yes," she whispered. "What are you—?"

"Doing driving a car?" He laughed. A raucous clatter of a laugh that ended in a spasmodic burst of coughing. "Gotta earn a crust. No one seems to want an old man with emphysema in on their game. Had to go legit. I sure wish your old man was still around. He was the best."

Sandy shut her eyes.

"You okay, Sandy?" She nodded. He coughed again. "What are you doing mixed up with those Danielis, anyway? You don't want to run a scam on cops. That's asking for trouble."

She opened her eyes and stared at him. He looked old. "I'm not running a scam on anyone. I'm just— I'm just—What do you mean *cops*?"

"You don't know? Old man Danieli is a captain up here. Hey, lucky you ran into me ain't it? What've you got cooked up, anyway?"

So Marco's dad was a cop. Why did that make her feel like she was guilty of something? She needed to stop feeling like a criminal when she was just a regular person these days. "I don't have anything cooked up, Joey. Never have. I couldn't stop my dad from breaking the law, but I have a job. I earn my money."

"Me too, now, more's the pity. Not too much of it, either. You telling me you're going there on a social visit?"

"Yes." She smoothed her dress again, now with really sweaty palms. A social visit. With a police captain and his sons? Her eyes instinctively closed again. The urge to retreat into her own little private zone was overwhelming.

"You seeing one of those boys? Nice kids. I like

'em all, but don't tell 'em I said so. And don't tell their dad what I used to get up to."

"There's no danger of that. Can we go?" *Before I lose my nerve. What frayed thread of it I have left.*

"Sure, Sandy. Geez, it's good to see you again. You kind of dropped out of sight there."

"Intentionally. I'm trying to build my own life now, and being Ralph Riley's kid isn't exactly a glowing reference."

"He was a good man, Sandy. He loved you. He did the best he knew how."

"Then why couldn't he stop drinking? Why couldn't he stop gambling? Why did he have to go and die in prison?" Tears stung her throat.

Ugh! She thought she was past this.

Losing her dad still hurt so much. She was so sure he'd be able to turn things around, that as an adult she could help him rebuild his life. She'd just graduated from high school, she planned to get a job and support them both while he got a handle on his addictions. But he couldn't say no to one more stupid con game. Even when he knew he'd never survive another stretch behind bars.

If he'd loved her he would have tried harder.

"I'm sorry, Sandy."

"Yeah, me too."

Joe was gabby. One reason he was a lousy crook. By the time they pulled up outside Gloria Terrace in Newark, she knew far more than she needed to about the comings and goings of the North Jersey underworld and its denizens. Not exactly the kind of information you want spinning in your mind as you sit down for dinner with a police captain.

Your juvenile record is sealed. You have a clean slate now.

You'd never know it from the way she flinched like a lab rat with an electrode if she saw a police cruiser in her rearview mirror or when a beat cop strode in her direction. Guilt must be built into her DNA.

And there was a cruiser parked right outside the house. Tilted at a rakish angle on the sloping driveway.

She took a deep breath and straightened her shoulders. She was planning to run a con, wasn't she? To convince the Danielis into thinking she was an ordinary girl.

Maybe she'd take it one further and try to get them thinking she was a "nice" girl. Not someone who'd grown up sleeping in the back rooms of bars and on the floors of other people's apartments. Hiding from the authorities who'd take her away for good if they knew her dad was locked up for another six months and her mom was long gone.

The cruiser took up most of the narrow driveway and she had to squeeze past it to get to the front door. A glimpse of steel handcuffs lying on the backseat made her stomach clench. Her heart thundered and her pulse pounded painfully in her temple as she rang the bell.

You're doing it, Sandy! You're brave enough not to run away.

She struggled to control her breathing as she listened to footsteps on the other side of the door. Marco opened it. At the sight of his broad smile, a wave of relief washed through her. Marco didn't feel like a stranger anymore.

"Come in." Grinning, he surveyed her from head-to-toe. "What a vision. You look lovely."

"Thanks." So do you, she thought. In a black cotton shirt tucked into faded jeans, he was irresistible.

He leaned forward and kissed her gently on the cheek, the way he'd done on their first date. Again her skin warmed under his touch, filling her with optimism and a sense of renewal. When she was with Marco, nothing seemed impossible.

He settled his hand at the base of her spine as he guided her though the narrow hallway into a brightly lit living room packed with people.

"Okay, so there are a few more people than I thought," he whispered in her ear. His smile tickled her neck. "Come meet my dad. I've told him all about you."

A stab of alarm chilled Sandy to the marrow. The startled glance she shot him caused Marco to raise his eyebrows and chuckle. "Okay, not everything." He winked. "Just the usual stuff, you know."

No, she didn't know. She had no idea. Maybe where she lived, what she did, that kind of thing? She took a deep breath and unconsciously smoothed her dress as Marco led her though the throng of chattering people.

"Hey, Dad, this is Sandy Riley, the girl I told you about. Sandy, this is my dad, Vic Danieli."

"Hello, Sandy. Nice to meet you." The elder Danieli was a big man with a shock of pale gray hair and the same steel toned eyes as his son. Sandy shook his hand with as much conviction as she could muster. She'd never shaken hands with a cop before. She'd been arrested by one, but that wasn't quite the same.

"Hello, Mr. Danieli," she forced out, in a voice

barely above a whisper. At that moment she was saved by the merciful arrival of a very large, very loud woman who hurled herself at Danieli senior and kissed him on both cheeks.

"Vic! Long time no see!" The newcomer quickly monopolized his attention.

Marco slipped his arm around Sandy's waist and led her back through the crowd. "Quite a turnout tonight. I didn't know the old man had so many pals."

Half of them probably cops, thought Sandy with a suppressed shudder. Upholding law and order.

Nothing wrong with that. She had nothing to be ashamed of, not any more.

Marco took Sandy into the kitchen where he introduced her to his two brothers, both tall and raven-haired like Marco. Danny, the youngest, was stuffing himself with homemade appetizers as they approached. "This kid never eats unless he's got someone feeding him. Struggling artist and all that."

"I'm an architect, Marco."

"Same difference." He winked at Sandy as Danny sparred with him playfully.

Marco's older brother, Steven, wore a police dress uniform, which once again made Sandy's heart seize with unwarranted terror as she shook his hand. "Sorry I'm decked out," his eyes twinkled with humor as he murmured his apology. "I got stuck with a fancy function tonight that I couldn't get out of. Thought I'd come over and get some of Aunt Louisa's home cooking before I headed there."

He seemed nice enough. Maybe most cops were just ordinary people with a job to do? Marco's face beamed as he watched her chat harmlessly with his brothers about the stadium Danny was designing, and whether the Mets or the Yankees were having a worse summer.

"Come upstairs," he whispered in her ear after some minutes of conversation. "I'll show you my old room."

Sandy giggled. She was a little jumpy, but she was actually enjoying herself. Marco surreptitiously slid his hand to her backside and gave it a quick squeeze as he pushed her gently toward the stairs. The sensation of warmth it created made a blush rise to her face.

"I hope no one saw that," she chastised, a smile tugging at her lips.

"So what if they did? Admiring the female form is no crime."

"Groping it in a crowd of your dad's friends might be."

"I'm a grown man. I can grope with impunity." And to prove it, he goosed her as they turned the corner on the stairs. Scandalized and aroused, Sandy leaped to the top of the stairs, laughing. Marco dashed up after her and grabbed her hand. He pushed open a door at the top of the stairs, and pulled her in.

"Alone at last." In an instant, his lips were on hers. The heat of their kiss sucked the breath from her body. Sandy wound her arms around Marco, giving herself over to the sweet sensation of coming together with him.

They were both breathless, eyes shining, when they finally managed to pull apart. Sandy glanced around the room and laughed when she saw it looked like it still housed a teenage boy.

"Your parents never redid your room."

"Nope. Embarrassing isn't it? I should come up here with a garbage bag some time." Sandy took in the sports trophies, the model cars, the cheesy posters. Paraphernalia of an ordinary adolescence.

So unlike her own.

"I'm surprised no one's cleaned it out by now. It must be years since you left." She looked up at Marco, and her heart stuttered when she saw his face suddenly taut with emotion.

"I suppose you're wondering about my mom." His voice was gruff.

"Not really." Perhaps she was dead and she'd just triggered a slew of sad memories. She was the last person on earth to ask where someone's mom was. She couldn't even find her own.

"My parents divorced when I was eight."

"I'm sorry."

"She couldn't deal with my dad's job. The hours, the stress, I guess it took its toll. She remarried."

"Do you ever see her?"

"Not much. She has kids with her second husband." Marco turned away from her and ripped down the poster of a girl in a wet T-shirt. "Dad raised us. He's my hero."

A knock on the door startled Sandy. "Yo, Marco, dinner."

"We'll be down in a minute, Dan. Don't eat all the sausages before I get there." He turned to Sandy. "At least he knows better than to just burst in. The kid is learning."

"It's funny you still think of him as a kid. I bet he's older than me."

"He's twenty-five," Marco's eyes widened. "How old are you?"

"How old do you think I am?"

Her body sizzled as his eyes roamed over her from

head-to-toe. But she couldn't help noticing his admiring gaze was shot though with alarm.

"I never thought about it. Geez, I guess I assumed you were in your late twenties when I first met you. But without the makeup—you look a bit younger."

"I'm twenty-four. Nearly six years younger than you."

"So? That's not so much. C'mon, let's go downstairs."

Marco held her hand as he led her back into the fray of guests, who were seating themselves along a row of card tables that had been pushed together and covered with red paper tablecloths. Seated, the crowd didn't look so large, maybe twelve or fourteen people.

"Sandy!" She jumped at the sound of Marco's father booming out her name. "Here, next to me." He patted the seat to his right. Sandy glanced doubtfully at Marco, who just winked at her and prodded her in that direction.

She squeezed out an anxious smile as she sat down. Vic Danieli offered to pour her some water and she nodded.

"Thanks."

"So you're from Jersey City?"

"Yes." Now she was. What else did he know?

"I grew up there. It's changed a lot, but it's still a great town. You always lived there?"

"Oh, more or less."

"What do your folks do?"

Think on your feet, Sandy! "They've both passed on." Of course her mom had passed on into the arms of another man, probably quite a few of them in fact. She looked down at her plate and prayed he'd drop the topic.

"I'm sorry to hear that. Roast beef?"

She helped herself to the aromatic meat and assisted in passing dishes up and down the table. She found herself totally unable to initiate a conversation with Marco's dad about the police force, and she didn't know anything else about him.

She forked a bite of macaroni into her mouth, then realized no one else had started eating. *Great, Sandy, why don't you just show them all you were raised by wolves?* She put her fork down and hoped no one would notice her blazing face. Marco caught her eye and smiled warmly at her. Perhaps he was enjoying the sight of her in the bosom of his family.

He was so confident, managed his complicated life with such ease, nothing seemed to worry him. It didn't occur to him that he might have brought a wolf into a pen of lambs.

There's nothing wrong with you, Sandy! You belong here as much as anyone.

Yeah, right.

Several people toasted Vic Danieli's advanced age and robust health before he interrupted to protest that his food was getting cold.

Everyone ate with gusto for a few moments, including Sandy, until Vic leaned toward her with a conspiratorial grin. "Sandy Riley. The name Riley takes me back."

Sandy's roast beef congealed to a solid lump in her throat.

A balding dark-skinned man from the far end of the table jumped in. "Wasn't he a prizefighter? Welterweight?" Sandy held her breath, hoping that was the one he was talking about. She didn't have any boxer relatives that she knew of.

"Dunno, never followed the fights. The one I'm thinking of…" The older Danieli smiled and shook his head. "Oh, that man led me on a merry dance over the years." He turned to Sandy. "It was back when I used to work in Atlantic City."

Her heart sank and her eyelids itched to close and shut out the scene, but she struggled to keep a poker face. Atlantic City. *Home, sweet home.*

"You wouldn't know him, but Ralph Riley was his name."

Sandy flinched. Her heart started to pound out a retreat. Every nerve in her body sang with the instinct to leap up and flee, but she held her ground. She took a sip of her water to avoid looking into his eyes.

"He had his finger in every small-time pie on the shore. He was never involved in the big stuff, the serious money, but if two thousand Viennese linen tablecloths went missing from a dock in Elizabeth and turned up in a banqueting hall in Trenton, chances are he was behind it."

Laughter boomed out, banging against Sandy's eardrums. She cringed, remembering the Viennese tablecloth debacle. Her dad probably only made a few hundred dollars on the deal, and the incident made him the laughingstock of North Jersey for months. But the police never managed to pin it on him, even though everyone knew he'd done it. Ralph Riley was slippery as an Atlantic City eel and proud of it.

"But I'm proud to say I finally nailed him. He was running a phone scam, selling phony insurance. Raking in the dough for the first time in his life. I was going crazy because I couldn't figure out who was behind it—though naturally I had my suspicions—"

He paused to take a sip from his glass of red wine.

He looked around the table, obviously enjoying the rapt attention of his audience. "It was a woman that handed him to me."

Sandy looked down at her plate. She remembered only too well. Her dad had insisted that people trusted a woman's voice far more than a man's, were less likely to be suspicious. He'd wanted Sandy to make the calls, had begged and pleaded with her, but she'd refused.

So he'd found a woman, Jessica Spavers, and trained her. She'd been a star, much to Sandy's disgust. On top of that her, father had fallen madly in love her. His adoration of her had made the sting of her betrayal and its consequences that much more fatal.

"When this woman was brought in for petty larceny and she revealed she was the one making the phone calls, I couldn't believe my luck. I hammered away at her for hours until she agreed to testify against him. She wanted a sentence reduction, I wanted Ralph Riley—the Hummingbird they used to call him 'cuz he moved so fast you couldn't catch him—so we struck a deal and boom, Ralph's back in the slammer—and with a ten-year sentence."

"Go Vic!" Glasses were raised in a toast that caused a wave of nausea to surge inside Sandy. She raised her water glass to her lips and put it back down as her gut curdled with disgust. She didn't care what they thought. She wasn't going to toast her own father's imprisonment.

Vic Danieli's chuckle made her gut twist. "The old bastard croaked behind bars. He's right where he should be now, down in the sulfur pits of hell with all the other small-time hustlers who gave me this ulcer."

He patted his stomach.

Sandy looked at Marco, who was eating, apparently paying little attention to the conversation. It was probably just more of his dad's shoptalk to him. His face brightened when she caught his eye, but a dark hollow appeared above his eyebrow as he took in whatever expression she had on her face. She turned to Vic Danieli.

"Ralph Riley was my father." She forced out the words in a harsh whisper. "He made mistakes, he made a hell of a lot of mistakes, some of them really bad ones. But he was my father and I loved him and I'm not going to sit here and listen to you dance on his grave."

Vic Danieli's mouth dropped open. "But he was—you know—white."

"Yes, he was. And my mother was black. I'm biracial." Could this get any worse? She looked up at Marco, who was staring at her in astonishment. "I'm sorry to spoil your party. I think I'd better leave now."

She pushed back her chair, careful not to knock it over, and nodded an apology to the rest of the table. Out of the corner of her eye, she saw Marco rise to his feet.

"Wait, Sandy—"

"I've got to go," she forced out. Tears gagged her as she snatched up her bag and hurried to the front door. She wrenched it open and ran out into the street. She had no idea where in Newark she was; she just needed to get as far away as possible. She ducked into a side yard. She didn't know if Marco would follow her—she didn't want to know—but she couldn't face him right now.

She ran past two tiny backyards and out onto the street behind. The street sloped downhill to a busy-looking intersection, and she walked briskly toward it. She could get a bus home or something. It didn't matter how long it took, no one was waiting for her.

She fought back the tears that burned behind her eyes. Damn. She'd been so close to being an ordinary person for a short while there. Invited to dinner with her boyfriend's family. Even the innocent necking in his bedroom was a taste of the free-spirited teen years she'd missed out on. And she remembered Marco's cheerful expression as he had introduced her to his father and brothers.

He'd be wearing a different expression now, all right.

How embarrassing for him. To be unwittingly dating the daughter of Ralph Riley, the mastermind of the Viennese tablecloth caper and the genius behind the All-American Life and Guarantee scam. She'd made him look like a fool in front of his whole family.

At least he couldn't say she hadn't warned him.

Salt tears pricked her throat, made her gulp as she struggled to keep them from spilling. She strode along the sidewalk with her head down, eyes hidden from the gaze of passersby. She'd known that no good could come of Marco getting mixed up with her. She was cursed to spend the rest of her life on the outside looking in. And she'd better not forget that again.

It took over an hour to find her way home by bus and train. An unseasonal cold front descended, chilling the air as much as her mood. It was late and the streets were deserted as she reached her block, shivering in her flimsy summer clothes.

She'd half expected to see Marco sitting on her

stoop as she approached, but he wasn't there. Then again, she wasn't surprised by that either. Maybe he'd finally come to his senses. She wasn't feeling too much of anything. She was numbed by the cold, by daring to dream and being so rudely awakened.

No Marco on the stairs inside either.

Had she really expected him to be sitting there, waiting for her? What a high opinion she had of herself these days. She must have some ego to think that one of the most important men in the telecommunications industry had nothing better to do than follow her around all day and night.

She slid her key in the lock and pushed the door open into the black loneliness of her apartment.

"You ran out on me again." The graveled voice emanating from the murky darkness almost knocked her off her feet. A whimper died in her throat.

Marco.

9

"Where are you?" She flicked on the light and saw him sitting on the sofa, elbows on his knees, hunched over, squinting at her in the sudden brightness of the overhead light. "How...how did you get in here?"

"Your landlady took pity on me."

His hair was ruffled as if he'd been running his fingers through it. He dragged his hand down over his face. "Why'd you take off like that? Why do you always have to run away?"

"You'd have wanted me to stay?" There was no disguising her surprise.

He looked hard at her, his voice quiet. "Would it have killed you?"

Sandy was silent. She looked down at the floor. She hadn't felt she had any choice but to take off when she did. Had she demonstrated yet another fatal moral failing? The inability to stand her ground and take her punishment? She'd had enough of being punished for the sins of others. She'd just as soon run if she got the chance.

But right now she had no energy left to run.

"I'm sorry I humiliated you in front of your family."

"You didn't humiliate me. My dad felt like a royal

ass, but he deserved to."

"I'm sorry I spoiled his party." She looked up at him, blinking in the brightness. Her heart crumpled a little more as she pondered what she was about to say. "Everything he said was true."

"He shouldn't have said it the way he did."

"How was he to know there was a con artist's kid at his sixtieth birthday party?"

"He shouldn't have spoken of anyone that way. Not a dead man." He rubbed one hand along his forearm, pushing up his shirtsleeve. "Cops get jaded, hardened, you know. It's hard for them to think of the people they...work with, as individuals, people like them."

Sandy heard a harsh laugh slip from her lips. "Not like them, believe me. My dad and yours have less than nothing in common."

"They both had kids they loved. That they raised and took care of."

Sandy shook her head and bit her lip for a second before replying. But there was no sense hiding the truth any longer. "No one took care of me. I raised myself. You have no idea of the things I've done. Of the times I've gone to the back door of restaurants, looking for food. Believe me, you don't want to know."

"Damn, Sandy, I'm sorry. I had no idea."

"I did warn you I wasn't your regular, average nice girl from down the block."

Marco raised his head and looked at her. She stood in the doorway, the door still ajar behind her. Her arms were wrapped tightly around her chest as if she was trying to hold herself together. She looked so frail in her light summer dress. Under his gaze she lifted her shoulders and tossed them back slightly, defiant.

Sandy was such a bizarre blend of frailty and indestructible strength, of mystery and allure, a source of both joy and pain. He didn't know what to say. Truthfully, her background and behavior scared him.

"Why are you here? Why don't you just let me go?" she asked. Her face was unreadable, a poker face, the face of a trickster. The woman who'd led him on, seduced him with her feminine artistry. She'd come to him in disguise, a con artist, playing him for a sucker.

"That's a very good question." He surveyed her through narrowed eyes, steeling himself against her. "Did you know that every woman I ever loved has run out on me?"

He rubbed a hand over his face. "You already know my mom left when Danny was a baby. One day she was just gone, and Steve and I were left to wipe Danny's little butt and dry his tears."

"My mother left, too." She spoke quietly. "I haven't seen her since I was little."

A stab of compassion rocked him. "It's a big thing, losing your mom." The emotion he was feeling right now scared him. "Maybe we're both damaged in some way that can't be fixed. Maybe that's why I fell so hard for Deanna. She was older than me. Just a few years, no big deal. But those few years made her impatient. It turned out she only loved me for better or worse until something better came along. Something inside me died the day she packed her bags and left."

At least he'd thought it was dead. Until he met Sandy.

He looked up at her. Her hazel gaze dropped to

the floor as his eyes met hers. His gut clenched with the longing to reach out to her, but she wrapped her arms around herself again. Keeping her distance.

"Maybe I'm doomed to be attracted to the kind of woman who'll love you and leave you. Dump you just when you're starting to trust them, run out on you when you needed them most."

He looked anywhere but at Sandy. He struggled to keep his eyes off her, to keep his wits about him. If he wasn't looking at her, if he wasn't thinking about her, he could almost pretend she was just another girl, another person, someone who didn't have any power over him.

But the moment he let his guard down he suffered a surge of terrible longing, a craving to touch her, to hold her, to share himself with her. He could feel the pull of her loneliness that called out him and echoed in his own bruised heart.

"I don't know what the hell I'm doing here—" He let the words drift away from him. "I guess I should leave now."

He wrested his eyes away from her and crossed the room in two strides. She was blocking the way to the door, but she stepped aside as he approached, crushing herself up against the kitchen counter.

Still, the space was so cramped that he had no choice but to brush against her. His fingertips trailed accidentally over the skin of her arm and a shockwave of sensation rocked him. He jerked away, stung by the power of her touch, aching with the loss of it as he pushed past her and closed his hand over the door handle.

If he left now, he wouldn't come back. And she wouldn't come after him.

Goodbye.
But neither of them said it.

As the door closed behind him, Sandy crumpled to the floor. She felt like a puppet who'd been held up by a single string, a single strand of hope. When Marco closed the door and the lock clicked back into place, that single thread snapped.

She listened to his footfalls on the sidewalk in the silence of the late night hour. She heard the sound of his car engine starting, of the car maneuvering out of its parking space. She strained to hold on to the fading purr of the motor as Marco drove out of her neighborhood. Out of her life.

She'd wanted so badly to fight for him. To convince him that this time things could be different. That they could make it work.

But she didn't really believe it.

A strange animal sound rose in her throat, a keening, that frightened her enough to gather herself up off the floor and try to get herself under some kind of control.

Marco left because he'd realized what she'd known all along. That she wasn't good enough for him. That she never was and never would be, even though she'd managed to fool him for a short time.

Goodbye, Marco.

As she tried to mouth the words, the awful high-pitched sound strangled her throat again and she clapped her hand over her mouth to try and contain it. Her heart squeezed and she gasped for breath, suddenly a fish out of water in this awful empty universe where Marco no longer existed for her.

Not even in dreams. She couldn't allow herself

that indulgence any more. Not now she'd seen the harm that came from letting her idle fantasies leak over into the real world.

As early-morning sunlight blasted through the slats in the blinds, Sandy pulled the pillow over her head. Even in the privacy of her dreams his name taunted her, his voice. It had been almost a week since she'd seen him, and each day had been hard labor in the solitary confinement of her misery.

It was getting worse. Now she was hearing his voice in her head.

"I realize it's the first time a civilian contractor has been given a project of this magnitude." You'd think if she had to be haunted by his voice that it would whisper sweet nothings. What was this babble? She must really be losing it. "We are confident that security risks can be eliminated. We understand the importance of this project in the interests of our national security—"

What the heck?

She peeked out from under her pillow and realized that Marco's voice was coming not from the depths of her tortured imagination, but from the tiny speaker on her clock radio.

She jerked upright and raised the volume.

"We've agreed to have our employees investigated to ensure the safety of all data and technology related to the project...." Good thing she'd left. She probably wouldn't have come out of an official investigation smelling like a rose, even if she wasn't actually guilty of anything other than sheer desperation.

"But we are confident that our technology will revolutionize the information-gathering processes of all government agencies and serve the interests of the country better than any of our competitors'.'"

Even reduced to a train of sound molecules that could travel though the wires of her radio, Marco's voice caused Sandy's stomach to twist into a knot. Her fingernails dug into the cotton sheets as she struggled to still her breathing. She didn't want to miss a single word.

"Thank you, Mr. Danieli. My guest was Marco Danieli, founder and president of Danieli Electronics, which is under consideration for one of the largest government contracts in the history of national security." She held her breath in anticipation of Marco's parting words. "Thank you." As the station announced the next story, she closed her eyes and sank back into the sheets.

Memories and dreams of Marco haunted her day and night.

She could almost swear she'd seen his car last night when she closed the curtains before going to bed. Parked down the end of her block, in front of the fire hydrant. But this morning she knew she'd imagined it.

Her imagination was becoming a dangerous liability. She'd better get it under control and get to work. Head out of the clouds and nose to the grindstone. That was the only way she was going to get her life back on track.

But after work she couldn't stop her feet from carrying her downtown toward Marco's apartment building. It was ten blocks south of the 33rd street office where she now spent her days doing data entry and filing old medical documents. She knew he wouldn't be there. She'd just get a little exercise, pick up a hot dog, breathe the fume-laden air. No harm in that.

It had been dark when she last came here as Marco Danieli's invited guest. Not as herself though, as her blue-eyed alter ego. And what a night they'd had.

She looked up at the gray façade of the old building, its big windows mostly curtained to keep out the prying eyes of the city. Marco's apartment was on the top floor, and she couldn't see more than the glare of the sun on his windows from down on the street.

Marco would be at work now, making multimillion-dollar deals that would shape the future of the country. He probably hadn't given her a single thought since the night he left her apartment and roared off into the night.

She closed her eyes, willing away the painful memory of his parting.

"Sandy." She heard his voice in her ear and squeezed her eyelids tighter. She was in the middle of the sidewalk, people striding past her in both directions.

"Sandy." Voices in her head. The torment of madness. She probably deserved it.

And then a touch. Fingertips on her arm. A sudden rush of adrenaline.

"Marco." He stood right in front of her, his broad body blocking the light.

"Are you okay?"

"I don't know." Was she imagining him? Was her mind so far gone that she'd conjured him, right here in broad daylight on a busy Fifth Avenue sidewalk?

She reached out to touch him, fully expecting him

to disappear. Her hand touched the stiff, white cotton of his shirt, and she snatched it back. She looked up into his face.

Dark shadows hung around his eyes, his cheekbones looked harsher, gaunt, as if he'd lost weight. And his eyes burned with a strange, tormented intensity. Their gray depths shone like molten metal hardening to steel.

They stood on the sidewalk together, not speaking, just staring at each other. Words choked her, wanting to spill out, but she swallowed them back.

Hold me. Hold me. Hold me.

The air seemed to hum with her unspoken plea.

"Sandy, what are you doing here?" Marco's voice sounded strained. As well it might. Stalked by a crazy woman. Hounded to his apartment by a grim apparition who wouldn't leave him alone.

"Walking." Her whisper was barely audible above the roar of the traffic and the buzz of passing conversations.

Marco raised his arm and she flinched, jerking backward. His eyes widened as he slowly placed his hand on her arm. The rich warmth of his touch soothed her, steadied her.

"Did you think I was going to hit you? Do you think so little of me?" His fleeting expression of surprise hardened into ire. "You've only told me a little of your story and I can see it's not a pretty one, but don't include me in the gallery of villains who've wronged you. I never did anything to hurt you."

"You left."

"Because you told me to. You left me first, remember? Ran out on me at my family home? I came after you. Don't know why. I must be mad."

His hand rested on her wrist. The warmth of his blood heated her skin as he closed his grip around it. "I am mad. I can't stop thinking about you. I can't eat; I can't sleep." His eyes danced back and forth, searching her face. "I've worked, done nothing but work, but it won't take my mind off...."

He paused, lips slightly parted, and Sandy's own lips stirred, softening in a mute response. Suddenly she was aware of their two bodies suspended in time and space, surging with life, urging them to...

"I'm sorry Marco, I..." She snatched her wrist from him and ran, ducking and darting through the agonizingly slow procession of pedestrians as she sprinted down Fifth Avenue. The wrong direction but it didn't matter. She needed to get away. To leave Marco in peace.

"Jesus!" His words exploded in her ear as he caught her around the waist in a tackle that shook the breath from her lungs. "You're going to make me chase you down a public street in broad daylight?" He closed his other arm around her, holding her fast from behind, crushing her body against his.

"You want me to chase you, don't you?" He squeezed her harder. "You enjoy the thrill of having me run after you. You want me to throw myself at you. That's the fun of it for you, isn't it?"

"I...I..." Sandy didn't know what to say. She only knew she didn't want Marco to let her go.

"You need me on my knees, begging, don't you?"

He released his punishing embrace and spun her around, gripping her shoulders with hard fingertips. "Well, you're not going to get it. I don't know what kind of game you're playing, but I'm not playing it any more."

The hell he wasn't. His chest tightened as her long lashes flicked closed for a split second, then opened to pin him with her warm gaze. Those wide eyes worked on him like neat whiskey, sapping his strength, drugging him. He wrenched his attention away from their hypnotic stare but it fell on her mouth, pink and ripe. He knew the taste of those lips, the intoxicating sweet wetness of her kiss.

She bit her lower lip. She had nothing to say to him. No words of apology. A sudden gust of wind tossed a curl across her face, and he instinctively raised a hand to move the hair aside. She lifted her hand at the same instant and their fingertips brushed each other.

A sting of electric energy shot up his arm and jolted his heart like a defibrillator. Suddenly, he couldn't think of anything but the glorious softness of her body, how it had felt to hold her, to fall asleep in her arms. The sheer joy he'd known the one time he woke up in them.

He loved this woman. He shouldn't, but he did. Cursed to love the wrong kind of woman and doomed to have his heart ripped from his chest, but he couldn't help it.

He softened his grip on her shoulders, and she didn't turn and run the way he'd half expected she would. He let his hands slide down over her back, pulling her closer. A sigh escaped him, audible, humiliating if he'd cared, as her soft chest bumped gently up against him.

Her eyes closed and so did his as he lowered his mouth. He needed to taste her, to drink in her essence and fortify himself after days and nights of lonely suffering. He needed to hold her. He needed—

As their lips met, a rush of sensation flooded his body. He tightened his arms around her and gave himself over to the explosive force of their kiss. He devoured her mouth with his, hungry, desperate with longing. He knew her hunger too as she squeezed him with her slim arms, tugging at his clothes, pulling him to her.

He rubbed his face against hers, releasing her scent, filling his senses with her maddening perfume. His hands roved over her thin shirt, itching to touch the warm skin that tempted him from beneath it. God, the feel of her was the drug he'd been craving.

A piercing wolf whistle jarred into his consciousness. His eyes kicked open, and he saw the laughing face of a bike messenger as he sped past them.

"We're on the street…." he managed. His grasp on reality had slipped, the blood departing his brain for other places where it was more urgently required.

Sandy's wide eyes revealed pupils dilated with desire. Her moist lips were still parted in a mix of shock and arousal. He realized with a jolt that he'd pulled her shirt out of her skirt and lifted it almost to her bra strap.

Jesus, he really was a madman.

He tugged her shirt down roughly. "We'll go inside." His voice was hoarse, with no trace of civility. He seized her hand and pulled her along the sidewalk back to his apartment building. He nodded and grunted to the doorman as he guided her toward the elevator. His mind was humming but not with defined thoughts. He wanted Sandy in his arms, with nothing between them.

In the elevator he lifted a hand to stroke her hair. "God, I've missed you."

"I've missed you, too. I tried to stay away."

"So did I. I couldn't though." He touched her soft cheek with his thumb. "I drove to your street last night. Parked at the end of it. I sat there all night."

He was losing his mind over her. Nothing she'd told him about herself made any difference. If anything, her raw upbringing made him want to protect her, to shield her from more harm. He wanted to hold her in his arms and keep her safe.

The elevator doors opened, and Marco unlocked the door to his apartment.

"Come in." He waited for Sandy to enter, then followed her, admiring the sweet curve of her backside under her fitted skirt as she walked hesitantly to the center of the room.

He shed his suit jacket. Thank God he'd left the air-conditioning on. He was burning up inside and out.

Sandy stood awkwardly in the center of the room. She crossed her hands over her chest, the defensive posture she assumed when she felt under siege. Was he going to lay siege to her? Damn but he wanted to.

He ripped off his tie and saw Sandy flinch. "I'm just getting comfortable. I won't strip myself naked and jump all over you." *Or will I?* He wasn't sure what he'd do around Sandy. And for someone used to being sure of everything he did, it was more than unsettling.

"Do you want something to drink? Water?" Her new nervousness prompted him to try and behave like a civilized man, not a horny Neanderthal who'd finally succeeded in dragging a woman back to his lair.

She nodded. "Water would be good."

He held a glass under the water dispenser and listened as the cool liquid trickled into the glass. Awareness of her eyes tickled the back of his neck. She was watching him, wondering, worrying.

Should she worry? Maybe.

He filled the glass, then strode across the room with it. Her eyes fell to his chest where his shirt was parted and he saw the desire that darkened them. She was in deep, too. Her gaze dropped to the telltale bulge in his pants and he made no effort to conceal the evidence of his lust.

Their craving for each other was mutual. And so was the fear.

Fear of what? Of exposing oneself, the deepest, most craven part, the loneliness. Of opening up to another person, making yourself vulnerable. Of being turned inside out and exposed to the vultures.

"I heard you on the radio," she said, looking at the glass he had handed her.

"Mmm." He couldn't help noticing the long, delicate fingers that held the glass. He wanted those fingers on his skin, to have them grip him, hold him, and—

"You were talking about a new contract. With the government, national security…."

"Yeah." His thoughts were becoming fogged again as his eyes settled on her mouth. A small mouth, begging him to plant his lips on it.

"It said that all your employees were being evaluated as security risks."

"Uh-huh." Her lids lowered momentarily, and he recalled the brush of those satin lashes against the skin of his cheek, how they'd teased his skin as her eyes rolled back in the throes of her passion.

"If I'd been there, I would have failed the test."

"Oh." His eyes fell on her chest, which heaved suddenly. The rise and fall of her breasts made his erection swell and he gasped with the urgency of his need.

"Marco! You're not listening to me."

"What?" He struggled to focus his attention on her words, to wrench his mind from the tormenting perfection of her body.

"Marco, I've been arrested, jailed. Being with me could jeopardize your contract."

He shook his head, trying to make sense of her words. Contract? Who could think about contracts when her slender waist beckoned him to wrap his arms around it?

"It's okay, Sandy. I don't care what happened in the past. It doesn't matter. The only thing that matters is you're here with me, right now. That we're together."

She looked at him warily. "But if the government found out you're spending time with...with..."

"With you."

"Yes." She looked down at the floor and swallowed hard. "They might not want your company to handle sensitive information."

"Who I love is my own business."

Her eyes leaped to his, wide with terror.

Had he just said what he thought he'd said?

"But...but..."

"No buts. Come here." He stepped forward and took her in his arms. She softened and warmed as he embraced her and held her against his body. His skin buzzed with electrical energy as it strained to touch hers. He lifted her shirt and wrapped his arms around the bare skin of her waist. His whole body ached with the need to hold her.

Her thighs shuddered against his, and he opened his eyes to see her face contorted with desire. On impulse, he grabbed her off her feet and swept her into the bedroom. He laid her on the sheets of the unmade bed where he'd lain awake night after night, longing for her.

"Lie still, relax, I want to pleasure you," he murmured.

Her lashes flickered and she bit her lip, acquiescing to his request. He removed her black pumps and took one of her stockinged feet in his hand. He lifted her foot and pressed his face into the delicate arch. He grazed the tender skin with his teeth and smiled as she shivered at the sensation.

He sucked her toes through the nylon, enjoying them like tiny ripe fruits. Her feet had been one of the first objects of his fantasy. After that first intoxicating night, all he'd had left of her was her sneaker. He'd been shocked by how his mind had strayed to wonder about the foot it belonged to.

He licked the sole of her foot and trailed his tongue along the back of her leg, painting a seam like an old-time stocking. His mouth rose to the warm crook of her knee and he pressed his face into the hollow, closing his eyes and reveling in the unique scent of every precious part of the body he loved and craved so much.

He held her leg high in the air as he pushed her slim skirt up to her hips and licked the inside of her thigh with his flickering tongue, through the taut fabric of her silky stocking.

Sandy quivered and released a small moan as he gently grazed his teeth over her throbbing sex, taunting the swollen flesh through its thin covering.

Nibbling and tasting, he pulled at her tights with his teeth, ripping the sheer mesh and tearing at it, a lion feasting on his prey. Sandy gasped as his wet tongue penetrated the rip and licked her bare skin, sucking and roaming over the flesh.

He placed his thumb over the hard pearl he could feel through her delicate panties and stroked it gently, and it throbbed beneath his firm touch. Sandy writhed and lifted her thighs, wrapping them tight around him.

His head trapped between her slender but powerful legs, Marco groaned. Her embrace pulled his face down over her sex and begged him to taste it.

His eager hands groped at the satin panties that covered her and pulled them down to reveal the rosy flesh he craved. He covered her with his mouth and sucked. The scent of her, the warmth of her, the aching desire he had for her, drove him to new heights of glorious madness as he savored the thrill of pleasuring her.

Her thighs still clung to him and her hands clawed at his hair as he relished the sweet taste of her. He grasped her buttocks, raising her hips and pressing his face into her as he felt the first wave of her orgasm ripple through her body. She softened her grip on him as she gave herself over to her climax.

She shook with the intensity of the sensation, her eyes squeezed shut and her lips parted in breathless ecstasy. He unbuttoned her shirt and pulled off the rest of her clothes. The sight of her beautiful body, naked under him, shuddering with desire, almost undid him.

His own arousal had passed the point of torment and was now a source of unbearable agony. His erection strained against his pants as he struggled to undo the zipper with fingers that no longer seemed to obey instructions from his brain.

Sandy's fingers joined his in the fight, yanking at the button at his waist, tugging on the zipper, and he knew she wanted him inside her as much as he needed to be there.

They shoved his pants and underwear down, and she tugged his shirt off as he fumbled with the protection. Her fingertips dug into the bare skin of his back as he seized her, pushed her gently back on the bed and settled heavily over her.

They both opened their eyes at the instant he entered her. She was so soft and wet that he slid right in, burying himself in the womanly depths that welcomed him.

He wanted to see her at that moment, and her gentle brown eyes spoke to him in a language his soul understood.

I love you, he read in their depths.

Words that he knew were echoed in his own steady gaze.

She wasn't running from him now, wasn't closing her eyes, trying to hide herself away. She was giving herself to him, strong and brave, daring to come together with him in the way only a man and a woman could.

The utter relief of burying his throbbing member in her made him groan with pleasure. It was good to be inside the woman he loved.

Marco lowered his face to hers and nuzzled her

gently, inhaling the scent of her. Her lips sought his and found his kiss. As he closed his mouth over hers, tasting and savoring, his hips fell into a rhythm that rocked them together.

The bumping of their bodies, the grinding of their hips, the swirling dance of their tongues pulled them together into a feverish dance of mutual excitement.

Sandy moaned and clawed at his back, and her uninhibited pleasure drove him wild. Strange guttural sounds escaped his lips as he sank into her and she rose up with him time and time again.

He opened his eyes again as the clamor of his orgasm racked his body like a train wreck, leaving him helpless and defenseless. Sandy's eyes rolled open as she gave herself over to the climax that shook her from head-to-toe, making her gasp and whimper.

He held her tight, wanting them to fuse together and become one so they could never be parted again. He couldn't bear to lose her; he couldn't live without her. She had his heart—she was his heart—and he knew he needed her as much as he needed air to breathe.

10

"I know your dad was a criminal. It doesn't matter to me," said Marco, as he spooned strawberry yogurt into Sandy's waiting mouth.

She swallowed the creamy mixture and licked her lips. Marco smiled, his eyes on her tongue. His admiring gaze—his loving gaze—warmed her. She felt relaxed, sensual, cared for.

But she couldn't seem to banish those tiny, niggling doubts that played around the edges of her consciousness.

Sure, he liked her now. He was aroused, intrigued, sexually satisfied—at least temporarily. He saw their life together only in terms of the possibilities. For Marco, no obstacle was too great to overcome. The world was his oyster, and the other pearls were just going to have to shift position to make room for him and his new love.

But Sandy didn't view the world with such wide-eyed optimism. She might have once. When she was younger she'd longed for the day when her mom would come back, when her dad would stop drinking, and they'd move into a little house with a white picket fence. She'd really believed that if she just wished hard enough, if she prayed and hoped and didn't give up her vision, it would come true.

Now she knew better. Wishing for something didn't make it happen.

Marco offered her another spoonful of yogurt, and she parted her lips to accept it. Again he smiled as she swallowed and licked the traces from her lips. His gray eyes were soft with wonder, the hard lines of his face bright with enthusiasm. He truly believed he'd found the love of his life, and they'd live happily ever after.

But he'd believed that before. And he'd been wrong.

"Marco, I know you care about me. And I, I…" She looked down at the sheets on his bed. Sheets where they'd held each other, clung to each other, and promised each other the world.

She looked up into his eyes and a swell of unnamable emotion almost choked her. "I love you."

She was brave enough to say the words. She did love him. She wanted so badly to believe it would be enough. But experience had been a harsh master for Sandy, and trust and faith were hard to come by. "I love you." She said it again, softly, letting the words drift toward him.

She saw her love reflected in the warm depths of his eyes. He believed her and trusted her. A coil of fear twisted in her heart. Was she worthy of his trust?

She looked out the window at the sun rising over the rooftops of the city. The rest of the world was waking up, too. The world where they'd have to find their place as a couple, as a family.

Her next words escaped her as a harsh whisper. "But I'm afraid."

"Don't be afraid, Sandy. I'll protect you." He put

down the bowl of yogurt and eased himself toward her on the bed. He settled his arms around her and held her close. The warmth of his skin and his healthy masculine scent enveloped her in a protective mantle that fulfilled his promise, at least for the moment.

"But who will protect you, Marco? My dad wasn't exactly America's most wanted but his story will come out. People will talk. My childhood was a mess."

He held her chin in his thumb and forefinger and tilted her face to his. "You're a strong woman, Sandy. You've survived a lot. Be strong for me. For us." Marco's eyes were dark with emotion. Sandy's heart ached with a humbling and powerful love that made her trust in their future.

"I will, Marco." And at that moment she really did believe that with their love, anything was possible.

The bright sunlight made her blink as they emerged from the dim lobby of Marco's building into the bustle of Fifth Avenue at morning rush hour. People shoved and darted past them, and Sandy felt dazed, as if she'd just stepped off a cloud and didn't know quite how to function in the real world any more.

"Mr. Danieli." A man leaped forward and seized Marco by the forearm. Sandy startled and instinctively dropped Marco's arm.

Marco didn't move an inch. "Yes."

"Gabe Raymond, *New York News*, might I trouble you for a comment on this morning's story?" His high-pitched voice and cockney accent grated in Sandy's ears.

Marco surveyed Gabe Raymond for a moment. "Would you care to tell me what this morning's story is?"

Raymond looked at Sandy, and a slight smile twitched at one corner of his mouth. "May I take your picture?" He lifted the camera hanging around his neck. "The two of you together?" His pale eyes gleamed with mischief beneath a mop of light brown hair.

Marco looked at Sandy and raised an eyebrow. "What do you think, Sandy, do I look pretty enough to have my picture taken?"

Sandy had watched the exchange in a kind of frozen terror, and words wouldn't form on her lips. Marco seemed relaxed, as if this sort of thing happened almost every morning. For all she knew, it did.

"What's the lady's name?" asked Gabe, adjusting a dial on his camera but not yet aiming it at them.

Sandy gulped. Marco calmly replied. "Sandy Riley."

"That's what I thought." Gabe's mouth twisted into an outright smirk as he raised the camera to his eyes and snapped a rapid-fire succession of pictures. Sandy attempted to plaster a smile on her face. She hoped her terror didn't show in her eyes but suspected it did.

Marco settled a reassuring hand on her waist. "So, Gabe, what's the big story? Why are you here?"

Gabe chuckled. "You are, squire. You and the lady."

"Must be a slow news day." Marco stood easily, head cocked, challenging Gabe to spill the story but appearing not to care if he didn't.

Gabe held his camera in front of his body like a cocked pistol. "We'll see about that."

Sandy tried to hold her shoulders square while

cringing inwardly. "What's the story?" she finally hissed at Raymond. She couldn't stand the way he was taunting them, holding all the cards and waiting for them to fold.

"Oh, just that Marco Danieli's gotten himself mixed up with a girl who's not likely to pass Pentagon security clearance." Gabe fixed his eyes on her. "A girl with a criminal record."

"I don't have a criminal record. I was a juvenile so the records are sealed...." She trailed off when her words came out more an admission of guilt than a denial.

Marco slid his arm around her waist and pulled her close. "All right, Gabe, that's enough. You've got your pictures, go have your fun. Sandy and I have work to do, like you. For the record, she's my lady. Now get out of here."

Gabe winked. "Thanks, squire." He backed away from them a few steps, then strode off toward midtown.

"Don't let them rattle you, Sandy." Marco didn't look at all put out by the encounter. "It's all in a day's work."

"Not for me!"

"I know. I'm sorry that my being a public figure is going to bring you publicity you don't want. I wish there was a way around it. You do get used to it though. I broke a couple of camera lenses before I realized it just goes with the territory."

"But he's not on your side, Marco."

"Sometimes they are; sometimes they aren't. Nothing much I can do about it. No sense getting an ulcer over it. C'mon, I'll walk you to work."

He settled a kiss on her cheek, and the warm touch

of his lips soothed and calmed her. Was it that simple? Marco let the troubles of the world roll right off him. Could she learn to do that, too?

Sandy deliberately avoided looking at newsstands as they strode uptown. When they reached her office building, Marco gestured at the newsstand opposite the entrance. Sandy's heart hammered in her mouth as she scanned the headlines. War, baseball, the commissioner of…there it was. "Danieli's Dangerous Dalliance." Marco chuckled as he picked up the paper and scanned it.

"Hey, I have fond memories of this moment."

He handed it to her and heat flooded Sandy's face as she saw them locked in the passionate kiss they'd shared outside his building the day before.

"How do they already know who I am?"

"Because that's what they do. Some poor slob was running around like a maniac last night putting this story together." He shook his head. "Kind of ridiculous when you look at what's going on in the world."

He put the paper back on the newsstand.

"Aren't you even going to read the article?"

"I'll be briefed on any news stories when I get to the office." Marco pushed her hair back from her face. She knew he saw her anxiety, and his eyes were soft with kindness. He kissed her gently on the lips, closed his eyes, and held her. Sandy let her own eyes close as his kiss stole her breath away and filled her with wonder at the connection that held them together.

"I wish I could keep you locked up in a castle and protect you from the world. I know your instinct is to run from anything that threatens you, but you don't have to run anymore, Sandy. You have to learn how to stand your ground. No one can do that for you."

She nodded, straightening her spine as she pulled back to look him in the face. "You're right, Marco. I've been hiding in the shadows too long."

"No more running, no more hiding." His fingers played over her hair again, tucking it gently behind her neck. "If you want to hide, then come hide under my wing, okay?"

She bit her lip and nodded. Marco wrapped his arms around her again. She buried her face in his shoulder, pressing against the stiff fabric of his suit, and let herself absorb Marco's comfort—and his strength—as he held her. Then she steeled herself to march through the rest of the day alone, kissed him goodbye, and headed into the building where she worked.

As Sandy entered the lobby she realized with a jolt that she was wearing the same dress she'd had on in the photograph. Its pattern of flowers and dots announcing to everyone that, yes, she was *the* Sandy Riley. Eyes seemed to follow her from all directions, staring, gawping, laughing at her.

As the security guard looked up from his desk and said, "Hi, Ms. Riley," she was sure she saw a gleam of mockery in his eye. Or was she imagining it? Why did she care what anyone thought? She should be like Marco and let it go. Focus on the things that mattered.

She settled into her morning routine of filing away the data she'd entered the day before. One of her coworkers kept the radio tuned to an all-news station, and Sandy was soothed by the steady hum of inconsequential stories about traffic jams and sporting events.

Until she heard Marco's name. It popped out from the hum of faceless voices and seized her attention. She froze in the act of opening a file cabinet drawer. Her breath caught in her throat and suddenly every cell in her body strained to hear the story.

"...A new complication for Danieli Electronics, which stood to capture the contract for upgrading and managing security at the White House and Pentagon with its voice-print technology. Questions are being raised in the Senate about Marco Danieli's personal connections to the New Jersey underworld."

The voice of the female anchor chimed in, "We'll bring you all the latest developments as they happen, with full coverage of all the breaking news, every hour, on the hour."

Sandy slumped into a crouching position on the floor as the station broke for commercials. Members of the New Jersey underworld? They made it sound like her dad was involved with the mob. And he wasn't. Well, not directly.

They hadn't mentioned her name, but it was only a matter of time. Already Marco's relationship with her was tarnishing the name of Danieli Electronics, undermining everything he'd worked so hard for.

Twenty minutes later she heard her name. And her father's. If it was television they'd be showing her mug shot from the one time she'd been arrested—and released when the charges were dropped for lack of evidence.

Sandy cringed as the two coworkers who shared her space in the filing room turned and stared at her.

"Sandy Riley? How many of those can there be? Is

it you?" Marie's eyes bulged behind her round glasses and her skintone suddenly matched her gray hair. Sandy nodded, swallowing hard.

"Holy cow!" Frannie pressed a manicured hand to her mouth, three-inch nails emblazoned with sunsets underscoring the drama of the gesture. "You're getting it on with Marco Danieli?"

Sandy didn't feel the need to dignify the remark with a reply. Her blazing face spoke for her.

"Still waters certainly do run deep, don't they, Marie? Who'd have thought? Little Sandy from Records and—well, there's no telling what some people find attractive. Not that you're not attractive, Sandy, but ..."

"Forget about Marco Danieli, what's this about you and the New Jersey mob?" asked Marie, her eagle eyes pinning Sandy to the filing cabinet behind her.

"I've never had anything to do with the mob. My father was a…well, he committed some crimes, but he wasn't in the mob. And I never had anything to do with any of it."

"That's not the idea they were getting across in that story."

"It's a slow news day," parroted Sandy, trying to convince herself.

She spent the next fifteen minutes fending off a barrage of questions about Marco and her relationship with him, and getting absolutely no work done. Thus it was almost fitting when her manager summoned her to his office with a grim look on his pasty face—and fired her.

He didn't mention the story about her and Marco at all. That might have given her grounds for wrongful dismissal. No, he blamed it on funding cuts, last hired/first fired imperatives—so sorry—two weeks severance pay, pack your things, and leave immediately.

Two weeks severance seemed rather generous since she hadn't even been there that long. It was a lousy job anyway. She'd find another.

She bid her coworkers a not-very-fond farewell and headed out onto the streets again.

The sun blazed down on her, blinding her as it glared off the windshields of passing cars. She wasn't sure where to go. She felt dazed, disoriented. The traffic roared in her ears, sirens screaming at the edges of her consciousness.

She started to walk north on Fifth Avenue, not because it would take her anywhere in particular, but because she was afraid that if she drifted south she'd end up outside Marco's building. He wasn't there, but more photographers might be.

She passed the window of a discount electronics store and the name Danieli caught her eye. A set of headphones for $59.99. She wondered what it must be like to see your name in random places, to know that products you had invented and manufactured played a part in people's daily lives.

Then the glowing image on one of the display televisions caught her attention—an image of Marco leaving the Pentagon, flanked by men in gray suits. Probably from a couple of days ago. Captions scrolled across the bottom of the screen. "Opposition in the Senate threatens months of negotiations. Danieli unavailable for comment as senators threaten to block security clearance." The image jumped to another story, but Sandy remained staring at the window.

Could Marco's big deal truly fall apart because of

his relationship with her?

The gaze of passersby seared into her. She cringed under their curious stares. She felt she should don a placard saying, "Yes! I'm that Sandy Riley."

She had the check for her salary and severance in her wallet, and she headed to the bank to cash it. All of her instincts were screaming for her to buy some different clothes, a wig, some dark glasses. To hide.

It was a lot of money. Enough to go away. Far away.

She'd never had that opportunity before. Usually she barely had enough spare change to do her laundry. As she left the bank her wallet bulged with almost two thousand dollars.

She felt like a bandit hauling a sack of swag. Especially since she hadn't actually earned most of it. The ill-gotten gains of her ill-gotten fame.

She could go to California—golden land of opportunity—and start again. No one would know her there, or know of her. She could go to Alaska and live in the wilderness. Well, maybe not. But she could move to Chicago or Atlanta or Miami. Almost anywhere, really. She was pretty generic-looking, so with a different name, a haircut, no one would recognize her.

Probably not even Marco.

At the thought of his name, her heart seized. Could she really leave him?

She could. It would nearly kill her but she could leave him. She could learn to live without him.

She could learn to live without her heart beating in her chest. Without hope, without love, with nothing to get her from day to day but the need to find the next meal. She'd done it before.

She knew what it was like to function as an automaton, denying yourself grief, sorrow, the indulgence of self-pity.

She pushed through the crowds, unthinking, unfeeling, her feet directing her toward the nearest PATH station. The clamor of the city blurred her senses, dulled her thinking. Possible futures unfolded in her mind like paper streamers that caught in the ocean breeze and lifted up out into the sky.

By the time she got home, she'd know what to do.

She wanted Marco to be happy, and there were many women out there who could make him happy. He deserved someone he could be proud of, someone whose accomplishments were in a league with his. Not someone who besmirched his reputation by her very presence in his life.

Tears pricked her eyelids and she gulped them back, unwilling to succumb to the terrible sadness building inside her. Marco didn't need her. He thought he did, but it was only the spell she'd woven around him—the allure of mystery, the thrill of the chase. She'd led him on and stirred him up far more than she'd intended to.

When the reality of life with Sandy Riley set in, he'd regret his ardent pursuit of her. He'd be sorry he'd let himself be led astray.

But if she went away the whole fuss would blow over and Marco's life would soon be back the way it was before. He'd be successful, well liked, respected.

And lonely.

The thought of Marco alone and lonely set her every protective instinct on fire. Made her want to run to him and hold him so tight he'd never feel lonely again. But being lonely wasn't the worst thing in the world.

It was better than being trapped in a relationship that would destroy his name and all he'd worked so hard for. A tear escaped her stinging eyelids and rolled down her cheek. She quickly wiped it away as she hurried down the stairs into the PATH station.

She cared about Marco so much. She wanted him to be happy. And if that meant she had to sacrifice her own chance at happiness, she could do it. She was strong enough to do that much for him.

When she reached her block, her chest tightened with horror. The street was packed with reporters. Television vans jockeyed for position, double-parked in the middle of the road. Reporters with still cameras jostled with video cameramen. Correspondents chattered into lenses in front of her building.

Sandy froze at the end of the block. It wasn't too late to turn and run. With two thousand dollars in her pocket, she could run and keep on running. She could leave her few belongings in her apartment. What did she want with sentimental mementos of a life that had brought her nothing but grief and regret?

They hadn't seen her.

Her feet itched to start sprinting. Her nerves sang with the call to flight. Go, go, go! The powerful instinct to flee, to run and hide, surged through her on a stinging wave of adrenaline.

But something else inside her held her steady.

This is it, Sandy. Fight or flight. And for the first time in her life, she knew she was going to fight.

11

She marched along the block, propelled by a sense of injustice. Filled with the conviction that no one was going to mess up her life and Marco's life—their life together—for the sake of a few entertaining sound bytes before a commercial break.

She pushed her way through the crowd of reporters thronging around her stoop. For a moment she wasn't sure any of them would recognize her. Certainly none of them were paying here any attention as she elbowed her way to the stoop. Maybe she could just climb the steps up into her apartment and no one would care.

"Sandy Riley?" A hush descended on the whole block, interrupted only by the rapid fire of a motorized camera.

"Yes, I'm Sandy Riley."

A mantle of calm wrapped itself around her as she stood on the top step and turned to face the crowd. A sudden barrage of questions assaulted her from all directions. She couldn't distinguish one from the next, and the roar of tangled demands and accusations sent a quick flash of anger surging though her.

"Stop!" She held up her hand. "Listen to me. I'm Sandy Riley, my father was Ralph Riley, who is now passed on and not involved in anything at all any more. Yes, I had a juvenile record from some things I got talked into doing when I was too young to know better or too scared to say no, but I'm a changed person today. I live an honest life."

She looked out at the sea of faces and a sudden realization of what she was doing—exposing herself to public view, to ridicule, humiliation and doubt— was like a splash of iced water in her face. But the iced water evaporated in the heat of her anger and indignation.

"I'm guilty of nothing more than loving Marco Danieli."

A surge of relief swept through her and threatened to knock her off her feet. Even if Marco turned her away now—if he thought better of their dalliance and sought to break their connection—she'd been true to herself.

For the first time in her life she'd stood up for what she believed in, and she wasn't going to run, consequences be damned. And that was a damn good feeling.

"And," she continued, "Marco's honesty and integrity, and that of his company, are in no danger whatsoever from any dealings with me. On his behalf, I resent and reject any trumped-up accusations made in the interests of filling page space and airtime."

Suddenly her attention fixed on a long, black sports car parked across the street, partially hidden by an Eyewitness News van. As she watched, the door opened and a familiar black-haired figure emerged.

Marco.

Her heart tripped, and her blood iced over like a river in winter. Who knew what had gone on in his mind since their last conversation?

He was here to personally control the damage. And what that would mean for her she had no way of knowing.

Time slowed almost to a standstill as their eyes met. His face was a mask, expressionless, his eyes fixed on her.

He shoved his way though the throng of reporters, his expression stony as flashbulbs made him blink and scowl. When he reached the stoop, she could see the fierce blackness of his eyes and what she read there made her blood slow to a glacial flow and her heartbeat rise to an agonizing thud, thud, thud that threatened to deafen her.

He reached out a hand to her. His mouth was a hard line, his jaw set. Fear kept her own hand at her side for a few moments before she lifted her agonizingly heavy arm and held it out to him. Tentative. Afraid.

He took her hand in his and a massive shockwave of blazing heat ricocheted up her arm, threatening to knock her off her feet. But the heat did not engender warmth. Marco's expression remained inscrutable, fearsome. Unnamable emotion blazed in his eyes as his grip tightened around her trembling fingers.

"We need to talk." His voice was low but not tender.

Her already constricted heart crushed a little further inside her chest.

Damage control.

"Your keys." He held out his other hand, and Sandy obediently handed them over. So different from the last time he'd asked for them and she'd refused. When she was still protected by her silence, by her secrecy.

Marco unlocked the door and pulled her inside. The hum of excited chatter disappeared as he slammed the door behind them. Alone with Marco in the dark, tight lobby of her apartment building, Sandy swallowed, words departing her.

Marco seized her by the upper arms and held her with a grip that dug into her flesh, scared her. The black storm clouds gathered in his eyes made her shiver with foreboding.

"Sandy…" Marco's brow creased as if he struggled to find the words.

I'm sorry.

We have a problem.

And the problem is you.

Her brain filled in the blanks left by his silence. The ice in her veins moved slowly, pushing sensible words to her lips. She'd led him on. She'd gotten him into this mess. It was nothing more than her responsibility to let him off the hook, to set him free.

"It's okay, Marco. I won't hold it against you." Her voice was so calm and controlled, so convincing, she barely recognized it as her own.

"Thank God!" His brow smoothed momentarily as relief washed over his features.

Sandy's blood chilled. Deep down she'd held on to a thin shred of hope that he wasn't here to cut her loose. That maybe he'd even come to claim her. With his exclamation of relief, that thin shred of hope drifted to the bare tiled floor to be crushed underfoot.

Marco's grip on her arm softened a little. If only his grip on her heart could do the same. His voice was so deep that the sound of it reverberated in her ears like a bass drum. "I wasn't sure you'd understand."

Oh, she understood. In the deepest recesses of her brain, in the microcosm of each cell in her body, she understood. The blackness and totality of her realization threatened to engulf her. She understood far too well.

His gaze remained steady, unblinking. His control perfect. "I wasn't sure you'd be able to accept it." As the rivers of ice pushed relentlessly through her body, she sought comfort in the fact that she was still standing.

Or was it only his iron grip that held her up?

"I'm stronger than you think." The control in her own voice surprised her. She was indeed stronger than she'd thought. And she'd need all the strength she could muster to get her through this. To help her survive while her heart was being ripped in two.

"I always knew you had that strength buried deep inside you. I could see it even when you couldn't." The tenderness in his eyes jolted Sandy and threatened to shove her off balance.

Don't show any weakness!

If only one of them was destroyed by this parting, it would be a victory she could cherish, a balm to sooth the raw hurt of her own pain. Because even now she loved Marco with her whole heart.

And she really did understand.

He'd been hurt before and knew better than to risk his whole life on a gamble that might destroy his company and leave him with nothing.

Marco's lips were tightly closed. Perhaps he didn't feel he'd have to say any more. That he could count on her to know the score. And he could. She'd warned him about the dangers of being involved with her.

"I'm glad you understand. That you can deal with it. I confess I wasn't sure how you'd cope. That's why I came here."

He took one hand off her shoulder, and Sandy stiffened her spine in an immense effort not to slump to the floor. Despair was beginning to melt her icy resolve. Marco reached his hand down into his pants pocket, underneath his suit jacket.

Oh God, he was going to offer her money. Hush money. Keep-quiet-and-go-away money. On instinct, she closed her eyes and pulled back from him. This was more than she could bear.

She wanted him to go away so she could nurse her pain alone. Or did she? The fingers of his left hand still held her right arm and even now the warmth of his grip steadied and calmed her. No, she wanted him to stay as long as possible. She wanted to savor every last second of their time together. Of their last time together.

"Sandy, open your eyes."

She didn't want to open her eyes and see the thick pile of banknotes or the crisp check signed with a flourish, the gesture of generosity that cheapened what they'd shared.

"Sandy." His hand left her arm and she flinched as the touch of his fingers on her jaw surprised her. His touch was so gentle, so soft—loving.... If only that were the case.

He stroked her cheekbone and pushed a strand of hair back of her face. "Open them, Sandy." And she did.

In his right hand, Marco held a small velvet box, opened to reveal a white satin interior that held the most beautiful ring she'd ever seen. A diamond solitaire flanked by two smaller stones, in a simple platinum setting.

Her eyes darted to Marco's face. His severe features glowed with excitement, his mouth curved into a smile as he watched her.

Confusion knocked the last vestiges of Sandy's senses from her mind.

A ring?

"Sandy," his voice was a little tentative, hopeful, but not overly confident. His hope, and his own fear, danced in his eyes. "Will you marry me?"

Shock and confusion dissolved into an understanding that shook Sandy from head-to-toe.

He hadn't come here to break their union; he'd come to seal it.

Hot tears stung her eyes. Her chest warmed and expanded as the sun rose on a new world of possibility. Intellectually she couldn't comprehend what was happening at all, but her soul understood. Her heart knew.

"I'll marry you, Marco." She bit her lip and hot tears dripped over her cheeks as Marco lifted the ring from the box and slipped it onto her finger. It fit perfectly.

"For better or worse," said Marco quietly, looking into her eyes, reading her reaction. "For richer or poorer…"

Sandy nodded. She knew what he was asking. He wanted the assurance that even if his company was destroyed and his wealth vanished, she would still love him.

And they both knew she would.

She whispered, barely able to form the words, "As long as we both shall live." Two more tears rolled down her cheeks and dripped off her chin, and she blinked, struggling to staunch the flow.

Marco lowered his head and his lips claimed hers in a kiss that warmed and softened her body. Her blood pumped hot and her heart filled, brimming with the love they shared, a love she'd never have to deny again.

When at last their lips parted, Marco pressed his cheek to hers and murmured in her ear. "I was so afraid this evil circus would drive you away, that you'd regret ever having met me. I suddenly had a terrible feeling you were going to run again."

He was right. That had been her first thought. Though now it seemed like a lifetime ago.

"I knew I couldn't stop you if you really wanted to go, but I had to try. When I saw the way you stood up for yourself, for us—"

Marco buried his face in her shoulder. "I was so proud of you at that moment. So hopeful—but I still couldn't be sure until I'd talked to you. Then when you said you understood—"

Laughter bubbled up and gushed out of Sandy like water from a mountain spring. "I thought you'd come here to break up with me! That's what I meant when I said I understood. I understood that you needed to get away from me—that you couldn't take the pressure."

Marco pressed his lips softly into her neck and she felt his smile curve against her skin. "The only pressure I'm worried about is the pressure of your body on mine and how I want to feel that kind of pressure for the rest of my life."

Sandy wrapped her arms around his chest. She could feel his muscled torso through the fabric of his suit, and the strength and steadiness of his body rooted and grounded her. Confidence crept through Sandy. Confidence in Marco, in their love, confidence in herself.

"I love you, Marco."

"I know. I really do. And I love you, Sandy, more than I thought was possible."

Sandy's body hummed with pleasure as Marco settled his lips over hers in a kiss that charged and fortified her.

"Well," he said, when they finally drew back to gasp for air, "I think we have an announcement to make." His eyes sparkled with excitement. There was no trace of worry or anxiety in his bearing. "Are you ready to face the vultures?"

Sandy nodded. With Marco at her side, she could face the hounds of hell and pet them on the head.

He settled his arm around her shoulders and, with a broad smile on his face, he opened the door onto the explosion of camera flashes and barrage of questions that awaited them.

EPILOGUE

"You can't see her before the wedding! It's bad luck." Conchita paused from blow drying Sandy's hair to scold Marco through the door. "Go away!"

"That's just an old superstition." Sandy wanted nothing more than a reassuring hug from Marco right now. "Please let me see him."

"No." Conchita pursed her lips, which were uncharacteristically pink with lipstick. Since she was such a loving tyrant, they let her get away with murder. "You'll see him at the altar where you'll become man and wife. And not a moment too soon!" She cast a knowing glance at Sandy's pregnant belly, then winked.

Sandy shook her head. They'd set a date for the wedding, giving them plenty of time to plan a grand affair, then discovered two weeks later that she was already pregnant. "I still think we should have waited. The dress would look so much prettier if my waist wasn't three times its normal size."

Conchita had sewn the dress herself from some of the most expensive fabric known to mankind: hand woven silk covered with thousands of tiny seed pearls. Marco'd encouraged her to let her imagination run wild and go nuts. She had.

"It's important to be married before the birth. To give your child a proper name."

Sandy sighed. She'd been an outsider long enough herself, and the object of cruel gossip, to want her child to have every advantage in life. "I suppose you're right, but it still seems very old-fashioned."

"Sometimes old-fashioned is the best way." She smiled mysteriously, still tugging at Sandy's hair with the brush while wafting the blow dryer, making it fall past her shoulders in a gleaming sheet. "If more people listened to old ladies, the world would be a happier place. Where would you be without me, eh?"

She had a point. "Who knows? That nasty manager probably would have fired me by now. I don't know what her problem was."

"She was jealous." Conchita stopped the dryer and smoothed her hair with a palmful of some mystery emollient. "She could see what I saw, that you were a beautiful young woman destined for great things."

Sandy raised a brow. "So both of you could tell that less than a year later I'd be living in a big mansion in New Jersey—with the owner of the company—just weeks away from giving birth to his baby?"

"While studying part-time at Princeton University." Conchita brushed imaginary lint from her shoulder. "And to think you wanted to refuse that date when I first offered it to you!"

"Why did you buy the raffle ticket in the first place? Did you realize employees weren't supposed to enter?"

"Pfft." Conchita winked. "My English is not so good-looking. And I needed some excitement in my life." She put down the dryer.

"You've got it now you've come to live with us."

Conchita had moved in to one of the twelve large bedrooms in their new house in Alpine, New Jersey, to help plan the wedding. And she was giddy with excitement about helping with the baby when it arrived.

Sandy tossed her hair, which looked like satin. "Am I finally done?" They'd been in here all morning. The woman gazing back at her from the mirror looked insanely glamorous, just as she had on her first date with Marco. Funny, really—he'd told her many times since that he preferred her natural look. Still, you couldn't argue with Conchita, because none of them would be here today without her energetic scheming.

"You look like an angel." Conchita pressed her hands together, admiring her handiwork.

"Luckily Marco knows I'm anything but." She stood and fluffed out the full skirt of her incredible dress. "Now is it okay with you if I just go marry him?"

"Of course, my princess." Conchita ushered her to the door. "I planned it that way all along."

THE END

ABOUT THE AUTHOR

Jennifer Lewis grew up in England where she enjoyed a steady diet of fairy tales—some of them quite unsuitable for children—from an early age. She is a USA TODAY bestselling author of more than thirty books and her stories have been translated into more than twenty languages. A New Yorker for many years, she now lives in sunny South Florida and when she's not sitting at her laptop she can often be found at the beach. Read more about her books and join her new release mailing list at www.jenlewis.com.

AFTER THE STROKE OF MIDNIGHT